UNTIL WE MEET Again

Until We Meet Again

by ELLE JAMESON PEARCE

OCTOBER 2018

UNTIL WE MEET *Again*

FOR MORE INFORMATION
PLEASE VISIT SETONPUBLISHING.COM
ISBN-13: 978-1-7325450-3-8
ISBN-10: 1-7325450-3-0
PRINTED IN THE UNITED STATES OF AMERICA

Dedication

For mom and dad,
who inspired this story

Until We Meet *Again*

Publisher's Note

The greatest pleasure a publisher has is publishing a new writer's book. Just seeing the proof copy will put a broad smile on a person's face, and sometimes make the tears flow.

Elle Jameson Pearce's delightful "Until We Meet Again" had been in print years ago but not in a distributable form. Recently she had read a book by Duncan McCollum, and the "Publisher's Note" impelled her to contact me.

Her decision led to minor editing on my part, and more importantly putting her in touch with my colleague, Michelle Manos, who reformatted the interior and designed the cover.

In "Until We Meet Again" Elle has told a charming romantic story about "real" people, people we might know, set in the period just after the Second World War in Nebraska, Montana, and the California Central Coast.

Elle wanted us to hurry this book into print because...she has a new book getting ready for the presses.

TONY SETON
Carmel, California

UNTIL WE MEET *Again*

One

APRIL 1945

It was a beautiful spring day as Jim waited for a ride to school with his best friend, George. He sat on the front porch of his parent's boarding house and lit his third cigarette of the day. 8:11, 8:12, 8:13—where was he this time, Jim wondered, as he impatiently glanced at his watch. "Want a biscuit?" his mother Bess hollered from the kitchen.

"No thanks, Ma. George'll be here any minute," he answered. Down the street, he heard the roar of an engine and glanced up. Suddenly, there was George with his big toothy grin driving a brand new 1945 Buick convertible. "Couldn't you have picked a brighter color?" Jim laughed as he admired the crimson paint and shiny chrome. "Afraid the cops might have trouble spottin' ya, buddy?"

"Shut up and get in, or we'll be late again," George said.

"Your old man got a case of the guilts?" asked Jim.
George knew what his friend was referring to and said, "Yeah, big time—I was downtown last week and saw him and that Bradshaw woman goin' into the Carlyle. I know he saw me too but pretended like he didn't. Next thing I know, we're car shoppin' for an early graduation present. Jesus, what a schmuck!"

"Gonna tell your mom?" Jim asked.

"Na," George replied. "She probably wouldn't believe me anyway, and with Joe just gettin' home from the war, she's got all she can handle."

Twin Peaks High School was a 1905 two-story brick building with creaky wooden floors inside and photos lining the walls with each of the graduating classes for the past forty years. The grounds were regularly manicured, and the front walkway was lined with poplar trees. It was just one of several buildings that were located within the town square. With spring in the air, the tulips and daffodils were resplendent, and the last of winter's snow had finally melted. George screeched into an empty parking stall and flung the car door open.

"Aren't you gonna put the top up?" asked Jim.

"Are you kidding?" replied George. "We're already five minutes late, and you know what that means—detention again!" God, Jim thought, how he hated that—hadn't they finished their last one just two weeks ago? Still, there was no one he wanted to hang out with more than George Chandler. They had been friends since grammar school when Jim had moved to Twin Peaks from Nebraska, and he knew they would remain friends throughout life. Yep, two peas in a pod, he mused to himself as they approached the entrance to the school.

Mr. Beatty, Principal of Twin Peaks High, was waiting in the doorway when Jim and George arrived. His scowl, which seemed a permanent fixture of expression, seemed even more rigid today. The two boys looked through the glass door, then at each other as they approached the top of the front steps, knowing what awaited them inside. "Mr. Riley, Mr. Chandler, how wonderful to see you again," he said with a forced smile. "Into my office, now!"

As they followed him down the long hallway, they knew there would be more retribution than just two weeks of detention. Mr. Beatty took his seat behind the large wooden desk stacked with files; and as the boys sat down, he glared at them over the top of his bifocals shrouded with heavy brows.

"You two are incorrigible," he began. "Do you know how many times you have been in detention this year?" Jim looked at George, trying to keep the smile off his face and began counting on his fingers while looking deep in thought. "Don't bother doing that," Mr. Beatty said. "I've got your records right here," as he grabbed two files off the top of the stack. "This time, though,

it's going to be different. During your two weeks in detention, you will stay an additional hour after school and help Mr. McKenzie clean all the restrooms!" Mr. McKenzie was the janitor and had been there since the school opened its doors. Although he was pleasant, his health was failing, which caused him to work at the speed of molasses in January.

Upon hearing this news, Jim and George looked at each other and knew they would be sacrificing an opportunity after school to engage in yet more fun and mischief. An alternative must be thought of, and quickly. Jim decided to go first.

"Mr. Beatty, you know my parents own that boardin' house over on 7th. Well, uh, you see, Ma works from sunup past sundown and needs me home by three thirty to help her get dinner ready for the boarders." At this point, Mr. Beatty's expression remained unchanged, so Jim decided to embellish in hopes of getting a reprieve. "My pa's not been feelin' well lately, and Ma relies on me more and more—I can't let her down!"

"And what about me?" George piped up, afraid he might be left holding the bag. "My grandparents moved in with us a few months ago, and I'm needed to help out with chores too! My dad's not home very much, and mom can't handle everything by herself!" He too had a flair for the dramatic when necessary.

Mr. Beatty sat back in his chair, removed his glasses (which was never a good sign), rubbed his eyes, and then re-perched the spectacles. He leaned forward and in a quiet voice that grew progressively louder said, "Guess what, you two? You both should have thought about that before being tardy again! Now, sign these slips, and your two week tour of duty starts today!"

As Jim and George left the office they were both racking their brains for a way out of this sentence. No way were they going to scrub toilets after school for two weeks. "Hey George," asked Jim, "how long has it been since we did the staring at the sun 'til our eyes turn red and watery gag?"

George thought for a moment and said, "Oh, 'bout three months ago, and Beatty won't remember it anyway 'cuz he was out with that hernia operation."

"Keen," said Jim, "we're outta here right after lunch!"

Two

Abby Lansing lived across town at the end of a street whose homes had fallen into disrepair as wives struggled to hold families together during the war. She was the first-born, and then came twin sisters, Nora and Cora, and finally her younger brother, Matthew (Mattie) who she adored. Her father, Kenneth, had sustained multiple injuries in France during World War I, and the cupboards of their home were lined with multiple bottles of prescription pain medications. If only those pills would make him even-tempered, Abby had often thought. It seemed as though they didn't ease his physical pain, either, as he frequently voiced his discomforts and all that he had endured these past thirty years. Her mother, Gretchen, was a long-suffering wife who worked full time, did her best to keep the household running smoothly, and endure her husband's ongoing complaints.

As a young girl of nineteen, Gretchen's mother had warned her against the marriage to an injured war veteran ten years her senior. Kenneth was recuperating at nearby Spring Hills Army Hospital where she was secretary to the hospital administrator. After work, she would often spend time visiting the wounded soldiers to offer encouragement. Her beautiful green eyes, flowing auburn hair, lovely smile, and curvaceous figure were a beacon of hope to many young men whose families were not able to be there for them.

When she walked into Kenneth's room for the first time, Gretchen was instantly attracted to his piercing blue eyes and muscular physique. After a brief introduction, she sat at his bedside and marveled at how easily they shared the details of their lives. She didn't notice that two hours had lapsed until the charge nurse appeared to check Kenneth's vital signs. "I'd better go," she said after the nurse had gone. Kenneth looked at her fondly and said, "Come to work early tomorrow and have breakfast with me."

She found herself staring into those eyes and stammered, "Well maybe," as it was all she could think of to say at the moment.

Gretchen had only been on one forgettable date up to that point. Her dream was to fall in love with a stable man, raise a family, and find contentment in her life. She would spend the rest of her days in a comfy bungalow style home in Twin Peaks, pursue her love of flower and vegetable gardening, have children, and grow old with a partner she deeply loved. Her own father had abandoned their mother and her five siblings when Gretchen was eleven years old, and it had scarred her deeply. She reckoned that explained why she had been on just one date at the age of eighteen—she had difficulty trusting men, in general.

The next morning, she arrived at seven o'clock at the hospital to find Kenneth clean-shaven and his dark hair neatly combed. He had ordered an extra tray for her. "You're terribly sure of yourself," she said to him with all the self-confidence she could muster at the moment. "How'd you know I'd be here?"

"Well," he answered, "a fella can dream, can't he?" She once again sat at his bedside, and they shared their first meal together. Even though it was bland hospital fare, it made no difference to them, as they once again began opening up to each other in a way neither had done before.

She glanced at her watch and said, "If I don't leave right now, I'll be late!"

As she arose, he grabbed her hand and said, "Gretchen, they tell

me I'm gonna be here for at least two months. Will you come and see me everyday?"

Just then, the place inside of her that did not want to trust a man seemed to vanish. She waited for the familiar internal feeling that told her to say no, but it didn't happen. "How about dinner tonight?" she said. "My treat."

After two months, Kenneth was discharged from the army and released from Spring Hills, and he and Gretchen married in a brief civil service ceremony at the Twin Peaks Courthouse. The first few months of their marriage were difficult as they lived with her mother until Kenneth was able to find work as a ranch hand outside of town. Six months later, they were able to move into a rented home at the end of Maple St. It was an older neighborhood and, at that time, the homes were well kept.

Summer arrived and found Gretchen outside tending to her flower garden that had been recently planted. Although she had dreamed of having children, she and Kenneth had been married for eleven years and not yet conceived. He was still working at the ranch and she at the hospital, and Gretchen continued to struggle with the reality that she might never be a mother.

The past month, though, she had suspected that her frequent bouts of morning nausea might be a pregnancy and had withheld telling Kenneth as she felt he might not be happy with the news. Lately, he had become moody and complained frequently. The local doctor had increased his doses of pain medications, and while that eased his discomfort, it did little to elevate his disposition. As she troweled the soil, she suddenly felt nauseated and had just enough time to run indoors to the bathroom.

When he arrived home that night to the smell of his favorite dinner, meat loaf and mashed potatoes, it made him smile in a way that his wife wished he would do more often. "Did you have a good day?" she asked.

"Yeah, we're breakin' in a new guy, but I think he'll get the hang of it. What's the occasion?" he asked.

"Does there have to be a reason for me to take off a little early from work and make dinner for my husband?" she replied. He noticed that she had brought out their china, a wedding gift from her mother, and the table had been set with linens and a vase of flowers from her garden.

He removed his cowboy hat and snuck up behind her, kissing the back of her neck. She turned around and kissed him gently on the lips. "I'm almost sure we're having a baby,"—the words came out before she could stop them. He stepped back from her embrace and stood there for a moment, looking stunned. "Well," he said, "guess I better see if Nate's got any more work he can give me."

When Abby was born, Kenneth seemed to enjoy being a father, and she was the first word he uttered when coming home from work each day. He would often take her out to the ranch with him, and she would brush the horses and fill the food pails.

It was four years later when the twins were born that their lives changed dramatically. Gretchen had not been able to stay home and raise their children as she had once dreamed. Her job at the hospital was the mainstay of the family's income, as Kenneth would not always be physically able to work. Her mother came to care for the children during the week, and would often remind her daughter about the extent of her husband's shortcomings and that she had told her not to marry him in the first place.

When Mattie was born two years later, Gretchen had hoped that having a son might make a difference to Kenneth. But, unfortunately, what seemed to matter most to him were his many bottles of pills. He

did, however, develop an interest in gardening, and they shared many hours outdoors together, planting, pruning, weeding, and watering. She often contemplated that this time they shared together had helped her endure the marriage. As the children grew, they continued to be the center of their mother's universe.

It was on an April afternoon in 1945 that Abby couldn't wait for her mother to arrive home from work so she could tell her the news. She had almost stopped by her office at the hospital on the way home from school, but hesitated because she wanted her mother's undivided attention. When Gretchen came home that afternoon, Abby was the first one to give her a hug and kiss. "Mama," she said, "the most wonderful thing happened today."

At that point, the other three children heard their mother's voice and came bounding from the kitchen. "Mama," said Nora, "I got an A on my typing test and Cora only got a B."

"Mama," asked Mattie, "Can I go ride my bike over to the new pet store? I heard they got a real boa constrictor!"

Gretchen was in the middle of congratulating the twins on their grades and telling Mattie "Yes, you can go, but be back in an hour," when Abby interrupted and said, "Hey, you guys, leave us alone for a minute, okay?" Kenneth was out of town on a cattle drive, and Gretchen had noticed how peaceful the house was in his absence.

She and Abby headed into the kitchen and sat down at the large table and chairs that Kenneth had built when they had moved here almost thirty years ago. "Well, what's your news?" Gretchen began.

"Mama, you know since I've been in high school, Jim Riley has always been intriguing to me. Well, I stopped by the Mercantile today to buy Mattie a birthday present. You know they've had that army soldier set in the window that he's been wanting for so long, and I finally saved enough money from working at the diner to buy it for him. The point is that Jim was in the parking lot across the street at the A&P Grocery, and I noticed he was staring at me while I was in the store. Really tried to pretend I didn't see him, but Mama, do you think he could ever be interested in me?"

Even though her mother knew that Jim Riley had a reputation as a ladies' man and felt her daughter was too good for him, she withheld her answer. Instead, Gretchen found herself fondly remembering that day in 1916 when she had first met Kenneth and knew exactly what Abby was feeling. So much had changed since then....She jolted herself back into the moment and said, "That young man would be a fool not to see how special you are."

Abby reached across the table, took hold of her mother's hand, and said, "Mama, please tell me the story again about how you met daddy."

Three

Jimmy Riley's parents owned a bar in Omaha and had sent him to live and work on a ranch about one and hundred and fifty miles away from them when he was seven years old. His father Jake and mother Bess had just lost their ten-year-old daughter Maggie to leukemia and were grieving deeply. They felt ill-equipped at that point to care for Jimmy and decided that he would be sent to live with his older cousin Mick Gallagher and wife, Blanche.

As Jake packed his son's belongings into the back of the Model A, Jimmy wondered if he would ever see his parents again. "Why are you takin' me there?" he asked his father.

"Well, we own this bar now, it's no place for a kid to be around, and your cousin could use the help. His wife's a real good cook, I hear. We'll be back to visit you in the summer." This was all the explanation that was given the boy, and before they departed, he had hoped that his mother might have kissed him goodbye. Instead, she reminded him to watch his manners and do whatever Mick told him to do, as they were doing them a big favor by taking him in. He and his father then drove in silence to O'Neill.

Upon arriving at the farm, Jimmy immediately noticed the pungent smell of manure—it seemed to permeate his entire body. "What's that smell?" he asked Mick as they unloaded the car.

"Oh, you'll get used to it," Mick answered. "Hell, I don't even notice it anymore." They made their way up to the farmhouse and Blanche had just started cooking dinner.

"Hi Jimmy—we been waitin' for ya. You like fried chicken?" she asked. "Hey Mick, why don't you show him where he's gonna be sleepin'?"

They made their way to a small bedroom in the back corner of the house. Jimmy noticed that even though the sun had not set, the air in the room was chilly. There was a small cot covered with a homemade quilt and an antique dresser with four drawers. A tattered area rug lay on the floor in the middle of the room. As he set his suitcase on the bed, Jake turned to him and said, "Why don't you unpack, kid, and come on out to dinner." As his father left the room, Jimmy sat there staring at the stark furnishings, and once again, for the second time today, his eyes filled with tears.

It was four-thirty in the morning, and he awoke to the clattering of pots and pans in the kitchen. He contemplated removing his long johns, but after feeling the icy temperature in the room, he quickly pulled his overalls on over them. Making his way to the kitchen, he realized the need to relieve himself and found Blanche bent over in front of the open oven door, shoving a pan of freshly made rolls inside. He stood there for a moment, and she turned around and said, "How'd ya sleep?"

"All right," he answered, "but I need to use the toilet."

"Well," she said, "better put your shoes on, 'cuz it's a little walk 'til you get there. Mick's been plannin' on puttin' one indoors, but that won't happen 'til after the summer harvest is over next year."

He stood there for a moment in disbelief and then realized she was serious. As he wandered back down the hallway to the bedroom, his young mind realized for the first time what awaited him should he need to do this in the middle of the night. Winter was fast approaching, and the thought of it chilled him to the bone.

"Jimmy, you ready to see what life is like here?" Mick asked, as they finished their breakfast of fried eggs and potatoes, washed down

with fresh cow's milk. "Follow me," he said. On the five-hundred acre property were one hundred dairy cows, mostly Holstein, two hundred head of Angus cattle, eight horses, sixty laying hens, twenty Berkshire hogs, ten goats, three dogs and two cats.

They headed for the barn, where the dairy cows were waiting to be milked. "Ever done this before?" Mick asked his young charge.

"No," Jimmy replied. "I've never seen one before, only in books."

"Well," said Mick, "sit down on this stool, put the bucket under here, like this." Although the large animal was at first intimidating, Jimmy found himself enjoying the experience for a while. In less than thirty minutes the novelty had worn off, and yet the sun had just begun to creep over the rolling hillsides.

Another ninety minutes passed, and his young hands were aching from the constant pressure on them to release the milk. "When do I leave for school?" he asked.

" 'Bout now," Mick answered, and Jimmy glanced up to find him headed toward one of the tractors. "Car's broke right now. I'll give you a ride today, but tonight, I'll give you some ridin' lessons on old Cherry and she'll take to you to school startin' tomorrow." He pointed to the corral just opposite the barn, and Jimmy knew he was referring to one of the horses inside that he had yet to meet. At that moment, he felt as though childhood existed only in dreams.

The schoolteacher, Miss Geraldine Hanson, was a middle-aged spinster whose only departure from O'Neill had been to earn a college degree. After graduation, she had returned and settled at the country schoolhouse and taught first through eighth grades. Despite her plain outward appearance, she possessed a love for her students and the community. Upon hearing the tractor pull up out front, she asked the students to continue studying their vocabulary words, and went outside.

"Geraldine," said Mick, "this here's Jimmy Riley. He's from Omaha, stayin' with me and Blanche for a while."

Jimmy, already fatigued from working for two hours and the three-mile tractor ride in thirty-five degree weather, approached his new teacher with all the energy he could muster. "Nice to meet you, ma'am," he said.

She put her arm around him, and Jimmy could not remember the last time he had felt affection from anyone. He looked up at her and smiled as she said, "Come on inside and get warm."

As Mick started up the tractor, he turned to Jimmy and said, "You can walk home with the Flaherty kids. They live down road from us."

Over the next seven months, Jimmy continued to rise every morning at four-thirty, milk the cows, and ride Cherry three miles to school. It was during these trips that he would dream of the city, of the life he once had in Omaha before his sister had died. During the heavy winter snow in O'Neill, school would be closed; and, after the morning chores, he would return and keep Blanche company in the kitchen. She had grown quite fond of the boy and was now expecting a baby in July. Jimmy found this very intriguing and often asked Blanche questions that she found a bit uncomfortable to answer. "How's it gettin' born?" Where ya havin' it?" he asked her.

"My friend Sally's a midwife," she answered, "and I'll be havin' it in our bedroom." She had hoped the questions would stop there and, thank God, they did.

"Why don't you come over here and help me pluck the feathers off this chicken?" she asked. Earlier that morning, they had gone out to the hen house to collect the eggs. Usually, Jimmy tried to avoid doing this, as the hens would peck at him and cause his fingers to bleed. Blanche had grabbed one of the chickens and headed outside, stopping

at a tall block of wood that had been secured in the ground. He had often wondered what it was for and glanced up to see her put the hen on the block, raise an ax, remove the head, and allow it to run around a few moments afterward. He stood there in the realization that this was both funny and sad.

Later that night as he lay in his bed, the young boy thought of his parents, whom he had not seen in seven months, and wondered what he had done to make them not love him.

Four

Jim and George managed to stay out of trouble the rest of the morning. Their class prior to lunch was woodshop. and just before the lunch bell rang, Jim was in the process of assembling the breadboard he had planned to give his mother as a birthday present. As the class ended, he and George darted out the door and stopped at the front walkway.

"Hey, remember last semester when you and I snuck into that room after school and glued everyone's projects together?" Jim laughed. "Yeah," said George. "I still can't believe they never figured out who did it. We didn't even get called into old man Beatty's office for questioning—it kinda took the fun outta doin' it."

"All right," said Jim, "we only have a half hour, so let's start starin,'" and with that the two began looking up at the sun for the next several minutes. Once their eyes were red and watering, they rushed back into the hallways shouting to see Mrs. Nash, the school nurse. They were escorted into her office by a couple of their buddies who were waiting inside to help execute the prank.

"Mrs. Nash," they began, "we were in woodshop workin' with some new kinda glue and accidentally rubbed it into our eyes!" She quickly had them dousing their eyes with water, as they continued to repeat how much pain they were in. Having been newly hired to Twin Peaks High, she was not yet aware of the boys' reputation and surmised that they needed immediate medical attention.

"Are your parents at home?" she asked. "I'm calling them right now so they can get you both to the doctor."

"Neither of us has a phone," said Jim. "I only live two blocks from here, so I can find my way home okay. My ma will know what to do, and besides, this is starting to feel a little better. "How 'bout you George?" Jim asked.

"Yeah, same here—I can walk home in five minutes."

"Nonsense," said Mrs. Nash. "I'll drive you in my car."

She stood up, covered each of their eyes with cold compresses, and escorted them both out to her car in the parking lot. She then remembered that she needed to sign them out with permission slips and said, "I'll be back in just a minute. Here's the key."

Opening the passenger door, Jim looked over the back seat at George and said, "Damn, I hope nobody's at home."

"Me too," said George. "I don't wanna have to explain this to anyone. I just need to get back here right away so I can pick up my wheels." Jim's reddened eyes had begun to fade a bit and he began smiling. "Hey," he said, "let's go skinny dippin' down at the hot springs!"

Fortunately, no one was home at either house. Mrs. Nash was hesitant to leave them there alone, but they convinced her their parents were never gone during the day for more than an hour. "Probably just grocery shoppin'," Jim assured her. As her car pulled away, the two waited for it to disappear from sight and began the walk back to school. They strolled leisurely so as to arrive after the lunch break was over and classes had resumed. As they unlocked the doors and got in the car, George pointed to the trunk and said, "I still have our swim suits from last time, if we want to put them on."

When they approached the hot springs, Jim couldn't help but wonder how many more times they would have the luxury of such folly. He would turn eighteen in a few days and had already received a notice to register for the draft. When the letter arrived, he remembered the frightening feeling that had come over him. So many of his upperclassmen had left Twin Peaks during the past three years and had been killed or seriously injured. Why can't I have flat feet and be exempt like George, he thought. His hope was that

Uncle Sam wouldn't send him any more letters, as he was looking forward to experiencing the world outside of this small town. He had been there for ten years now and had invited George to go to a business school in Omaha right after they graduated.

"What ya thinkin' about?" George asked.

"Nothin' much," Jim replied, not wanting to get into a serious discussion at the moment. "Hey," he asked, "you know much about Abby Lansing?"

"Why?" George replied curiously.

"Oh, I don't know," said Jim. "She just seems different than the kind of dame I'm used to bein' with."

George looked at him, arched his eyebrows and said, "You better leave that one alone, buddy, she's not your type."

"What's that spose to mean?" Jim retorted.

"Two words, my friend," George said. " 'Virgin' and 'studious.' And besides, you've seen her around for years—why the sudden interest?"

Jim's expression took on a serious tone. "I went to the A&P to get Ma some groceries for dinner yesterday," he began. "When I was comin' out of the store, I saw her through the window, shoppin' at the Mercantile. Buddy, I gotta tell ya', she was wearin' this light blue dress and with that red hair—well, it was all I could do to get in the car before she saw me starin' at her. Guess I just never noticed what a knockout she is!"

George looked at his friend in awe. He had never heard him say things like this about a girl before and wasn't quite sure where this conversation was going. The two already had a reputation of being womanizers and neither had ever been in a serious relationship.

At that moment, a voice inside George's head told him that what had been was about to change.

UNTIL WE MEET *Again*

Five

Jimmy Riley continued to work through the end of the following summer. Blanche had given birth to Bud, a healthy boy, and Jimmy looked forward to the end of the long hot workdays in the fields when he could finally return to the house and feed the little tyke his bottle at suppertime. The birth had been a difficult one, and Jimmy was grateful that he had been tending the cattle with the ranch hands that day.

Since his arrival last fall, he had already helped Mick with the birthing of several calves. One of them had been stillborn, and later that night he had cried alone in his room thinking about the ordeal. In some ways, it had reminded him of how grief stricken he had been when his sister died. His parents were dealing with their own pain, and he had felt alone and rejected.

Before Maggie's death, his mother would sometimes display affection towards him, but his father had never done so. His outward demeanor was gruff, and he rarely smiled. Christmas arrived shortly after Maggie died, and there had been no exchanging of gifts at home, just the usual holiday dinner. The day afterward, Jake had come from home from work for a lunch break. His father was at the refrigerator door, when Jimmy entered the kitchen. "Hey kid," he said, "here's a quarter. Why don't you go into town and buy yourself something," he said as he flipped the coin towards his son.

During the past ten months of working on the ranch, Jimmy had received two letters from his mother. The second letter arrived in July, and he was informed that Jake and Bess had sold the bar and were moving from Omaha to Twin Peaks, Montana to run a boarding house. They should be in O'Neill by next month with all their belongings, and Jimmy would once again be starting school in a strange place. Knowing this had filled him with fear, yet he was relieved that the long hard days of work would soon be over. He would miss Blanche, as they had become close in a way he had never known with his own mother.

It was the last week of August and Jimmy was just finishing baling the hay. He heard a car approaching and the sputtering of an engine. As he glanced up, he saw his mother waving to him, and hurried across the field to open the gate. He noticed that she was smiling, too. "Maybe she's not so sad anymore," he thought.

"Hey Jimmy," she said, as the car door opened. "Well, let's have a look at you."

During the past few months, he had grown accustomed to frequently hugging Blanche, and she would often give him a goodnight kiss before he went to bed. At first, this had felt strange to him, yet over time, he welcomed the fact that she made him feel special. He was thinking about this and found himself running over to his mother and throwing his arms around her. She patted him lightly on the top of head, released herself from his hug and said, "Say hello to your father."

Jake stood a few feet from the boy and said, "Well, Mick wrote us that you been a big help around here. That's good, 'cuz once we get to the new business, there's gonna be lots of work to do." Being tender in years, Jimmy hadn't realized just what owning a boarding house entailed. "Yep, we'll have to get up real early in the mornin' and start cookin', " he said. "Lotta laundry and dishes, too."

When he had learned they were moving, Jimmy had hoped to resume the kind of life he had in Omaha, before Maggie died. He would get up at seven o'clock for school, and the house would already be warm from the coal-heated furnace. As he dressed, the smell of his mother's cooking would waft its way down the hall to his bedroom. After school, he and Maggie would walk home, change clothes and play with the other neighborhood kids until their parents arrived home from work.

Today, as the impact of his father's words settled, he knew that his only hope at that moment was to find a real friend.

The drive from O'Neill to Twin Peaks took two days. As Jimmy sat in the back seat of the Model A, he envisioned his first day at the new school. During the past year, he had enjoyed Miss Hanson's class and had become one of her best students. She had done her best to encourage the boy she thought of as endearing, with a kind heart and a quick wit. He seemed to enjoy being with the other children, and she surmised that during school hours might be the only time he interacted with other young ones. He would arrive on horseback with his books and a lunch prepared by Blanche, his cousin's wife.

"Hi ma'am," were always the first words he uttered. "Got leftover fried chicken today from home, canned green beans, and fresh-baked cornbread." Miss Hanson would smile at him, knowing that at recess, Jimmy would share his food with those children whose families were still struggling to recover from the depression years. She knew that his stay out at the Gallagher farm was temporary, and it saddened her to realize that the little spark of sunshine she looked forward to each day would soon be gone.

They arrived in Twin Peaks on August 22nd, and the first order of business was meeting with the former owners of the boarding house, Fred and Marge Windsor. The home was a three-story Victorian that had been very well maintained. The outside was painted mint green with crème colored trim, and the flowerbeds had been newly planted with iris and primroses. In the middle of the front lawn was a grouping of birch trees, and there was a wooden sign hanging over the porch that read "Windsor's Castle." There were nine bedrooms, which included three in the basement, a large living room, parlor, kitchen, dining room and three baths. Jimmy nearly jumped for joy on seeing indoor plumbing and also noticed that even though it was very warm outside, the temperature of the interior rooms was quite comfortable.

"Built in 1886," Fred said "and solid as a rock. We're full up most nights, except durin' the winter. 'Spect the word gets out in town that the Mrs.

here serves up some good cookin'," Jimmy slowly glanced over at Marge. She looked tired, drawn, and her posture was slightly stooped. He thought of an expression he'd heard Mick once use to describe his neighbor's mare—"She's been ridden hard and put away wet," and it reminded him of the downtrodden lady that now stood there in the room.

They finished the tour of the home, and Fred went upstairs to fetch a stack of papers for the new owners to sign. Jimmy glanced out the window and noticed a boy about his age ride by on a bicycle. He had longed to own one—yes, it had made him feel grown up that Mick let him drive a car and a tractor on the ranch. But he wanted to experience childhood again, and, during the past year, had almost had forgotten what that felt like.

"Ma, can I go outside while you finish up in here?" he asked.

"All right," said Bess, "but don't wander off. We need to go downtown and get some dinner after we're done."

Jimmy went out front and sat on a wooden bench at the side of the porch. He reflected for a moment and realized how much he had missed living in town. That he would once again be starting school as a stranger was mitigated by the relief he felt to no longer be living at the ranch. His parents had told him he would be expected to do chores, but he had high hopes they would be very different than the grueling ones he had been doing this past year.

He glanced up and saw the same boy again, headed home with a sack of groceries in the basket of his bike. "Hey, you new around here?" he asked Jimmy.

"Yeah, my folks just bought this place, and we're movin' in tomorrow." Name's Jimmy—what's yours?"

"George," the boy replied. "George Chandler. See 'ya around," and with that he sped off down the street just as the sun was setting over the top of Twin Peaks.

Six

Abby awoke early the next morning and lay there in the stillness. She and her mother had been able to talk uninterrupted for an hour last night. Gretchen had once again shared with her daughter how magical life became when she first met Kenneth. "I would get up earlier than usual and take extra time getting ready," she told Abby. "I wanted him to keep looking at me the same way that he had the first time we met."

"But Mama, even now you're still naturally beautiful," said Abby. "And I've seen pictures of you back then, and it looks like you're wearing only lipstick!"

Her mother smiled and said, "Usually I was dear, and my hair was much longer too. I tried to change the style a bit each day. It was just one small thing I did to help break the monotony your dad felt during those two months in the hospital. When I came to visit him in the morning, he would look at me as though I hung the moon." At that moment Gretchen's thoughts trailed off and she tried to mask the disappointment in her marriage that had crept into her soul years ago.

"When did you know you were in love?" Abby asked.

Her mother searched deeply for an answer, trying to remember the time when she and Kenneth knew only the joy of being together. "I loved him from the moment we first met," said Gretchen, "and it didn't matter to me that he was wounded and recovering in the hospital. Even though our family backgrounds were so different, he and I were two kindred spirits."

"So you didn't marry daddy because you felt sorry for him—being injured and everything?" asked Abby.

Her mother looked intently at her and then said, "Dear, the only reasons to marry a man are that you are truly in love, and are good for each other. So many people marry for reasons other than that, but I can tell you honestly, when your dad and I said our vows, we became one person."

"But things are so different between you now," said Abby.

"Well," Gretchen replied, "sometimes things happen in a marriage that no one can predict. We're all just people, trying to find our way. And what happened in our past, when we were children, stays with us when we're grown ups. Remember when I told you that your dad was raised in an orphanage and felt abandoned by his parents? He had always hoped they would show up one day and take him home, but that never happened. He wasn't given hugs or praise, and he went into the Army when he was only seventeen years old. He didn't get to be a normal boy. I think that's why it was so easy for us to talk when we met, because my own dad abandoned us when I was only eleven."

"I know, Mama," Abby said, "when you told me that I couldn't understand how any father could do that to his own children—didn't you tell me that he left one day for work and never came back?"

"Um..." replied Gretchen. "There were seven of us including mother, and my sister June was only eighteen months old! But I had one thing growing up that your dad didn't, and it was a mother who loved us all very much. She was so generous to other people in need, even though we often had very little food in the cupboards and our money jar was empty. Your Grandma Hazel is a survivor, and she taught us to be hard-working and kind to others. God, I wished she lived near to us. I miss her every day, and if she were closer, my mother and I would be talking just like you and I are doing right now."

Seven

Until July of '44, Hazel Barrymore had lived in Twin Peaks her entire life. She was crocheting when the phone rang and was greeted with, "Hey sis, it's Genevieve. I didn't want to break this to you on the phone, but I've had all the tests and need to have back surgery. It's scheduled for next week, and I'm going to be laid up for a while. Can you come for a visit? I could really use the help."

She lived in Santa Cruz, California, a small town along the Central Coast. Hazel had been used to living in an area with seasonal changes, and Twin Peaks was gearing up for some very hot summer days. Her sister assured her that the temperate weather was well suited to "seniors," and Hazel agreed to fly out in two days. Her biggest regret was saying goodbye to her beloved daughter and grandchildren.

Gretchen had just arrived home from work when her mother phoned and asked if she could stop by and bring dinner. "Mama, you don't ever need a reason to visit," her daughter said. "Well," Hazel replied, "I'm never quite sure what's going on with Kenneth, and don't want to come over on one of his 'bad' days."

Gretchen didn't attempt a rebuttal—deep down she knew that her mother spoke the truth, as she had always done. She had been without a man in her life for thirty-six years, and Gretchen was her only child that lived in Twin Peaks. Hazel's other five children and fourteen grandchildren were scattered across the country. She was retired now, but kept busy with volunteer work and wished that circumstances had allowed her to spend more time at her daughter's home. "Mama, Kenneth's working late tonight at the ranch—did you by any chance make pot roast?" asked Gretchen, which was her mother's specialty. "How'd you guess?" she replied. "Six o'clock ok?"

Hazel arrived bearing pot roast with gravy, red potatoes, and carrots. She had also made homemade bread, tossed green salad, and the ever-famous dark chocolate cake for dessert. When her car pulled up out front, all four grandchildren ran out to give her a hug and kiss. Hazel knew that she would be gone indefinitely, so the embraces were all the more special. They held hands going into the house, each one helping to carry the dinner.

Gretchen was at the front door, looking tired but wearing a big smile. "Thanks for doing all this, Mama," she said.

"Thought you could use a night off," said Hazel while kissing her daughter on the cheek. After the sumptuous repast, Gretchen reminded the kids that it was time for homework.

"Before they go," said their grandmother, "I need to tell all of you something." Her daughter looked puzzled, sat quietly, and listened as her mother then told them that Aunt Genevieve needed help when she came home from the hospital and didn't know how long her recovery would be. "I will miss you so very much while I'm gone," she said. "Let's make a promise that we'll write each other, and I'll try and call you as often as I can." All eyes at the table began to fill with tears, and Hazel hugged her daughter and grandchildren harder than she ever had.

Eight

Jim and George finished their two-week detention after school. After all, how many excuses could they continue inventing and hope to graduate in two months? It was Friday afternoon, and they decided to stop by Hopkins Diner for a chocolate malt. "I'm buyin'," said George. "Now don't we got somethin' to celebrate—no more scrubbin' toilets!"

"Oh yeah?" Jim countered. "Have you forgot my folks own a boardin' house? I'll have john duty 'til the day I'm gone!"

They had been nearly inseparable for ten years, and when George's older brother Joe had gone off to war, Jim had filled the void he'd left. There were other guys they hung out with, but he didn't feel close to them. With Jim, he could just be himself, didn't have to pretend or hide anything, and he knew his friend felt the same way about him.

George had finally decided to go with Jim to Omaha right after graduation. Jim had assured his friend that they could work their way through school as hotel bellmen. There were plenty of big band orchestras that were lodging while traveling the country, and the tips would be generous. "Besides," he had said, "it'll give us a chance to experience the world beyond Twin Peaks. I lived in Omaha when I was just a kid, and it sure beats anything we have in this town."

As they entered the diner, Jim suddenly stopped and tugged at George's coat sleeve. "What's wrong with you?" asked George.

Abby Lansing was at the end of the counter waiting on a customer. "When did she start working here?" Jim asked.

"How would I know? We haven't been in here lately," said George.

He noticed that his friend was now hesitating and said, "Can we sit down please—this is spose to be a celebration, remember?"

They made their way to a booth, and Jim purposely turned his head away from the counter, fearful he might begin staring at her as he had done in the store parking lot last week. He was partially blocking his face with his hand and heard her say "Would you like to see some menus?"

As he glanced up, her blue eyes captivated him, and George quickly answered, "Na, we're only havin' chocolate malts, right Jim?"

As she walked away, he quietly said to his friend. "Buddy, you gotta get ahold of yourself. You'll never get to first base actin' like that!"

Jim tried hard to regain some composure before she returned.

"Will there be anything else?" she asked as she set their order on the table.

"No thanks," said Jim, "just the check." He had wanted to say, "Yes, there is something else—would you go out with me?" But to say those words would be reaching for the stars.

She was different than the others, he knew that. If he had asked her for a date now, she probably would have said no. He needed to take this slowly, and hopefully, in time, win her over.

"Well, what's your next move?" George asked him, glancing over at Abby.

"I need to think about it some more," Jim answered. "Now that I know she works here, maybe I'll stop by and try talkin' to her—hell, she could already have a guy for all I know. But I hope she doesn't—I want to ask her to the dance this Saturday night." So much for takin' it slow, he thought.

The next evening, Jim strode into the diner wearing his best buttoned down shirt and slacks. He had even polished his loafers, much to his mother's surprise. When he arrived, Abby wasn't there and he felt disappointed—so much that he decided to leave.

As he approached the door, she arrived with her beautiful auburn hair pulled back in a chignon and lipstick the color of amethysts. He marveled

that she even looked beautiful in a waitress uniform and then struggled to speak.

"Hi, my name's Jim...Riley."

"I know," she said. "Are you by yourself?"

He surmised that she was accustomed to seeing him with George and said, "Yeah, just me. Thought I would order some dinner. Only problem is, I don't like to eat alone."

Knowing what he wanted her to do Abby said, "Actually, I'm off work right now. I just came back because I forgot to grab my coat when I left."

Jim gathered all the courage he could muster and said, "Will you have dinner with me?" She smiled, and as they sat down, he felt that he was the luckiest man alive.

When Abby arrived home late, her mother was waiting for her in the living room. "Where have you been...I've called everywhere and no one knew where you were."

"Mama, I'm sorry" her daughter replied. "I meant to call you, it's just that the time got away from us."

"Us?" Gretchen asked.

Abby hesitated, and then said, "Jim Riley came into the diner after I got off work and asked me to have dinner with him. I meant to call you, but we just kept talking and the next thing we knew, Tom asked us to leave because he was closing for the night."

"Dear, you know what that young man's reputation is—he can't commit to just one girl. Is that what you want?" asked Gretchen. Her daughter's expression grew defensive as she said, "I know what you think about him. But Mama, he's different than that. And funny too—he made me laugh so much I didn't have time to finish my burger!"

"What happened after dinner?" her mother asked.

Abby knew that the answer she was about to give might not be well received. She took a deep breath and replied, "He asked me to the senior

dance, and I said yes."

This was the first time her daughter had made an important decision independently, and Gretchen was worried. Abby was a wonderful young woman…in spite of the marital friction that existed in their home, she was well adjusted, focused, and loveable with a smile that was contagious. Her mother could not contemplate Jim Riley being a suitable fit for her eldest daughter, and she was concerned that he would end up hurting Abby, using her until he moved on to his next fling.

But her little girl had grown up—she was already eighteen, and her goal was to leave Twin Peaks after graduation and move to California. There was an excellent nursing program there, and earlier this year her grandmother had decided to permanently relocate to Santa Cruz. She had sold her home in Twin Peaks, purchased one with an ocean view near Twin Lakes Beach, and had invited Abby to live with her while she was going to school. Genevieve had fully recovered from her surgery, so Hazel could once again enjoy doing the volunteer work she so loved and was looking forward to doting on her granddaughter once she arrived.

Gretchen stood up, walked across the room, and took hold of Abby's hands. "Since the day you were born, I've wanted you to be happy. I've had my say about Jim Riley—you've got a wonderful future ahead of you and my hope is that you don't lose sight of it."

"I won't, Mama," Abby said. "Just trust me, that's all I ask." And with that she leaned over, kissed her mother goodnight, and went upstairs to bed.

For the first time in her life, Gretchen reflected on a conversation twenty-nine years ago with her own mother when she informed Hazel that she and Kenneth were engaged. She realized that her daughter needed to be given the chance to begin spreading her wings and secretly hoped that after their first date, Jim Riley would become history.

On that night, she had no idea he would become the most important man in Abby's life.

Nine

Jimmy Riley awoke on the first morning in his new home to the smell of his mother cooking breakfast. Even though he knew there would be daily chores at the boarding house, he was grateful to be off the ranch and living in town again. This was his first day of third grade at Twin Peaks Elementary, and he was both excited and nervous—he thought of himself as a "country boy" and worried about fitting in. Heck, he didn't even own a bike and wasn't sure that he would be getting one anytime soon.

He wiped the sleep from his eyes and wandered down the hall to start the bath water. This bathroom was quite large with a beautiful claw foot tub that had copper piping and solid brass fixtures. As the steam rose from the tap, his mother appeared at the foot of the stairs and told him he needed to leave for school in half an hour. Jimmy plunged into the tub and lingered for a moment. He hoped that this was the last time he would be uprooted and forced to start over at a different school, have to make new friends, and leave old ones behind. He wanted to run, play, and do the things that normal eight-year-olds do. Most of all, though, he wished he could feel that his parents loved him—maybe it will come in time, he thought.

He finished the bath, washing his hair with bar soap and drained the water. He owned two school outfits and opted for the corduroy pants and knit sweater. Even though it was late August, the early morning weather was chilly, and he guessed he might be walking to school. He neatly combed his hair, and as he appeared in the kitchen, his mother turned from the stove and gave him a sizing up.

"You lookin' forward to your first day?" she asked.

"Yeah," I guess so," he replied.

"We'll drive there today," she said, "on account of I need to get you registered." He sat at the table and began pouring syrup on the pancakes she placed on his plate.

During the year on the ranch, he had forgotten what a great cook his mother was. He never remembered seeing her use a recipe—she would open up the cupboards and refrigerator, and minutes later a mouth-watering meal would be served. He thanked her for breakfast and the two of them drove to the school.

"Where's Pa?" he asked.

"He had to go into the hardware store to get some plumbin' stuff to fix the third bathroom toilet—it's gotta be ready before we can start rentin' out the rooms. The old owners told us it was busted and gave us a few dollars to buy the parts to fix it," she said. Jimmy mused to himself that he had just left a home in the country that still used an outhouse and now lived in a home with three bathrooms!

His mother had just parked the car when Jimmy heard a tap on the passenger window. It was George, the boy he had met two days before.

"Jimmy, right?" he asked. "Come with me and I'll show ya around." "Howdy, Ma'am," he said as extended his hand to Bess. "Name's George Chandler." And with that the two scurried off and up the stairs into the building.

"Do you know who your teacher is yet?" asked George.

"You mean you got more than one third grade?" Jimmy asked, incredulously.

"Well," said his new friend, "we actually got one that's just third grade and another one that's third and fourth combined. I'm not smart enough for that one," said George. "Truth is, I just don't like goin' to school, and I especially don't like doin' homework! Do you like school?" he asked Jimmy.

"It's been hard 'cuz I've moved around a lot," he replied. "This is my third school so far." George seemed puzzled by this, so he quickly added, "but I think my folks are stayin' put for a while."

As they walked down the first hallway, George pointed to his classroom. "I got Mr. Dutton this year. I've heard he's okay, but tougher than my last year's teacher, Mrs. McNally. Prob'ly won't be able to get away with as much fun stuff."

"What'd ya do?" asked Jimmy.

"I kinda like practical jokes," George said. "There's this girl Sharon Beatty, the principal's daughter. Thinks she's better 'n everyone else. Last year, I used to sneak over to the bicycle stand during recess and let the air out of her tires. Or, I'd go back to the classroom, open her lunch pail, and throw in a rubber snake or a live insect." Jimmy started laughing, the first time in ever so long, and George continued, "Yep, the little princess never did catch me at it either."

Just then Bess appeared in the hallway and said, "Well, Jimmy, you're all signed in. You can go ahead and walk home—it's just a couple of blocks. Here's your lunch."

"Thanks, Ma," he said and continued on with his new buddy. "This one's the third/fourth class. Mrs. Turner is really nice, gonna have a baby soon."

For a moment, Jimmy flashed back to Blanche and wondered how she and the new baby were doing. Wonder if I'll ever see them again, he thought.

George continued the tour adding, "Now this here's the cafeteria and up there's the stage. Last year the school had a concert and sang a whole bunch of songs up there, but I pretended to be sick that night and got out of it—that stuff's too cornball for me!"

Right now, George appeared to Jimmy almost as a character from a book—a rogue with untold adventures yet to experience. There had been a few mischievous boys in O'Neill, but his workload had excluded him from that kind of fun. With his new-found friend, he felt there was a lot of catching up to do. He was going to enjoy living in Twin Peaks.

Ten

Four days after Jim and Abby had dinner together that night in the diner, they were getting ready for their first date. The two hadn't spent any more time together that week as Jim was home recovering from a cold. He had phoned Abby on Friday to assure her that he would be there to pick her up Saturday night at seven o'clock.

He was taking her to dinner at Kay's Supper Club, famous for its fresh seafood. Abby had been there just once before, when she had turned eighteen in February. Her parents arranged it as a surprise, and they all dressed in their Sunday best. Kenneth had been in a rare congenial mood, which made the evening all the more special. After dinner, they had given her a pair of small amethyst earrings, her birthstone, and she was fondly remembering how wonderful the celebration had been. She was excited that she and Jim would be having dinner at this elegant restaurant and had been busy these past few days with all the preparations for their special evening.

After school on Thursday, she had driven forty miles to the Macy's store in Helena, as they had a large selection of formal wear. She was browsing when the store clerk approached. "What's the occasion?" she asked Abby.

"The Senior Dance this Saturday," Abby replied. "First date with a new guy—actually he's a dreamboat."

She stopped for a moment and thought that it was actually her first real date. Her friend Patricia's boyfriend had introduced her to Russ Sinclair at the Orpheum Theatre earlier this year and the four of them sat together and watched a Bette Davis movie. Afterward, they had gone out for a burger, but she wasn't attracted to Russ. She found him rather dull, and he was not very conversational. He had phoned her a few days later and asked her out, but she given him the "I'm busy" excuse and he didn't call again.

She resumed looking at the merchandise when the sales clerk appeared with the most beautiful dress Abby had ever seen. "With that auburn hair of yours, this color would be perfect!" she said.

Even though Abby had thought of buying one in a spring color, this gown was beautiful dark green velvet with a round neck and a plunging V shape in the back. Got to get a new bra to wear this, she thought. It was trimmed with rhinestones around the neck and down the back. The shoulders were padded, and it had long, tapered sleeves.

Noticing her look of approval, the clerk asked, "Now, let's go find the perfect shoes and evening bag to accompany it."

One hour later, Abby left the store and headed back to Twin Peaks. The excitement was building, that she could not deny. She stopped downtown at Emma's Hair Salon and made an appointment for Saturday. "Manicure too, please," she requested. As Abby drove home, she reflected that within the past two hours, she had spent a two-week paycheck. Would have spent double that if I'd had to, she thought, and it was at that moment the realization set in that her date with Jim Riley meant a great deal to her. She only hoped he felt the same way.

Jim awoke at five o'clock Saturday morning. His cold had settled down to a mild cough, and he was grateful for that. As he lay there in bed, he was reflecting on the past ten years of his life in Twin Peaks. He and George had remained the best of friends—actually, he's more like a brother, Jim thought. They had other casual friends too, but no one else really understood them. The two had formed a bond of fun and mischief, each covering for the other whenever the need arose. Jim knew that he would be spending less time with his good buddy if he developed a relationship with Abby and felt a fleeting sense of loss. Gotta find him a steady girlfriend, yeah, that would fix it, he surmised.

George was supposed to attend an out of town wedding with his

family this weekend and told Jim he wouldn't be there for the dance. He had sensed that George was almost relieved not to be going.

"Who would I ask anyway?" he'd said. "After all, the girls I date aren't exactly the kind you take home to meet mama, are they?" Until a few days ago, those were the same kind Jim had dated too, but he was so smitten with Abby and wanted to break away from that now.

When he phoned her the day before, Gretchen had answered, and he surmised that Abby's mother was less than pleased about their date. Still, she managed to be cordial and Jim had felt butterflies when he heard Abby's voice on the line after not seeing her these past few days.

Yesterday, he had reserved a tuxedo at Mitchell's, the first one he had ever worn. He felt that tonight was going to be special, a night he would always remember. Why do I feel this way now, he thought, when I've known about her for years? Oh sure, he'd seen her around school, but they ran in different circles and only shared a few classes together.

And then the "big" question invaded his thoughts. "Could I be in love? Does it really work like this sometimes? Do you see a girl across a parking lot, have dinner with her, and know she's 'the one?' Because I haven't been able to stop thinking about her, does that mean she's 'it' for me?"

With all these thoughts swimming around inside his head, there was little doubt in Jim Riley's mind why he was awake so early on a Saturday morning. He couldn't wait for tonight, couldn't wait to see Abby, and couldn't believe she said yes.

UNTIL WE MEET *Again*

Eleven

Abby was abruptly wakened by the phone after spending a rather restless night. She had been unable to sleep beginning at two a.m. as she pondered how the day would play out, but more importantly, the details of her first date with Jim. She knew the 'type' of girls he had dated in the past—what if he expects me to...? Her mind raced with the thought of it as she gazed out the bedroom window at the full moon. The stimulation of other thoughts continued. Why am I so attracted to him? He may go off to the war at any moment. He's so incredibly handsome and could have asked a dozen other girls to the dance.

The phone call was from Hazel, asking to speak to her "favorite red-haired granddaughter." Abby put on her robe and went downstairs to find Gretchen cooking breakfast.

"Hi, Grams," she said, as her mother handed her the phone.

"Heard you have a hot date tonight," her grandmother quipped.

"You've been talking to Mama," said Abby. "Yes, he's quite the deal and Grams, I bought the most beautiful dress in the world!" She then proceeded to give Hazel all the details down to her choice of jewelry.

"If only I could be there to see you—make sure your mom takes lots of pictures. For now, I'll console myself knowing you'll be here in August to register for school."

It just then dawned on Abby that she was leaving Twin Peaks in a few months, and, for the first time, she felt herself wavering. I'll deal with that later, she thought quickly.

"I wish you could be here too, Grams, and I miss you. See you soon," and she hung up the phone and rushed upstairs to begin a very important day.

Jim arrived promptly at seven p.m. wearing a black tux and a matching fedora hat. He came bearing a beautiful gardenia corsage, and when Gretchen answered the door, she found him inspecting his shoes.

"You must be my daughter's date," she said. "Just a moment and I'll go and get her." She walked upstairs to find her oldest daughter looking radiant.

"These are for you to wear," her mother said. "They were a gift from your Grandma on my wedding day."

Abby looked down as Gretchen opened her hand to reveal a pair of diamond studs. "Oh, Mama, they're beautiful…I love you!" replied her daughter with a hug.

"He's downstairs waiting, this Galahad of yours," said Gretchen. "Just remember who you are and what's important, okay?"

"I will," Abby reassured her and she walked down the stairs to find Jim looking up at her. He took hold of her hand without saying a word.

"This is for you," and, as he gave her the corsage and pinned it on her, he said, "You're stunning!"

When the front door closed, Gretchen watched from the upstairs window as they drove away, and once again, dreamed of bygone days. She was interrupted by the sound of her husband coming home through the back door.

"You just missed saying goodbye to your daughter on a very important night," she said.

"I tried to get here on time," he retorted. "Got behind one o' them slow movin' trucks on the highway, couldn't pass him."

Well, maybe you should have left earlier, she thought to herself, but chose not to voice it as she didn't want to get into a quarrel with him. "What do you want for dinner?" she asked and began reaching for the frying pan.

Twelve

The Supper Club was bustling when Jim and Abby arrived. He had called ahead for reservations, and arranged for them to be seated near the window with a view of the mountains that were silhouetted in the approaching darkness. The restaurant was candle-lit, and several of the customers were their own classmates dressed to the nines. Jim noticed that some of the older men were admiring Abby. *She's the most gorgeous one here, in this town—hell, in the world,* he thought to himself.

"Thanks for arranging this," she said. "It's beautiful."

He paused for a moment and said, "No—*you're* beautiful Abby...every man in this room has his eye on you. But if they try anything, they'll have to fight me first!"

"Hey, slow down cowboy," she said. "We're not in Hannigan's Bar, you know," she said smiling.

"My reputation precedes me," he replied. "Yeah, I've thrown down a few there. With so many guys goin' off to war, they bend the rules on our age. Guess they figure some of us won't come back, so they let our boys enjoy themselves while they can."

"What do your folks think about that?" she asked, and observed that his face took on a sad expression.

"They've never said, and I've never asked," he replied. "My sister died when I was a kid, and they ain't been the same since. Sent me to live and work on a ranch when I was seven. Didn't see them for almost a year."

As he uttered these words, he was looking downward. She sensed his pain, reached over, and took hold of his hand. He looked up and smiled.

"Hey, enough about me. We're out here to have some fun and laughs. Check out this menu, Abby. Now this is some restaurant, eh?"

They both ordered the poached wild salmon, served in a light lemon sauce. It was delectable, and during the meal, their conversation was as light as the entree. After all, they were just getting to know each other, and the two of them were still uncertain as to where this was going. As for Jim, he knew that he wanted her in his life, at least until he left for Nebraska as he hadn't thought or planned beyond that. Abby was captivated by his charm and good looks, and knew that she was moving in August to pursue her career. But, for this moment, this night, everything was perfect.

They arrived at the dance and Jim hopped out to open her door. As they entered the room, he felt his heart pounding. Several turned to give them a second look, but he tried his best to appear unaffected. He was with Abby, and that's all that mattered to him. The band began playing *Until We Meet Again,* and he asked her if she wanted to dance outside under the full moon. As she pressed her cheek close to his, he couldn't find words to express his feelings as the song echoed in the background…

My world changed
The day I met you,
Been re-arranged
Now it's all new.
There's a smile in my heart
Where there once was none,
I realized from the start
You were the one.
So darling hold me fast
And make this moment last,
For tonight I pray
That you could always stay.
I know the day will come
When we must say goodbye,
Until we meet again
With moonlight in the sky.

When the music ended, they went back inside to find George with a girl that Jim had never seen before. "Surprised to see me here?" he asked Jim. "This is Carla—we met last night at Hannigan's."

As they made their introductions, Jim noticed that George's taste in women hadn't changed. His date was wearing a very revealing dress and more makeup than he'd ever seen on anyone.

"Tonight's gonna be a blast, right buddy?" George asked with a mischievous grin. For the first time in their friendship, Jim wished that he could be on his own, without any interference from George. "Don't worry about the punch there buddy, I took care of spikin' it for us!"

Jim wanted to whisk Abby out of the room…she probably thinks I'm an idiot, he thought. As he turned to her, she gave him a warm smile. Well, maybe everything's still all right he thought, sighing.

"Listen George, Abby and I are gonna go dance some more….we'll see you two later." And with that, he grabbed her hand, and they headed onto the dance floor.

As midnight approached, they both realized that their special night would soon be over. Abby had promised her mother to be home no later than one o'clock. They had danced every dance, laughed, and intimately shared their dreams.

"After I graduate, if the war doesn't call me up, I'm leavin' for a business college in Omaha," he'd said. She told him that she would be moving to California in August to pursue a nursing career. They ended their final slow dance and he helped with her wrap.

"Chilly outside… better put this on," he said as he draped it over her shoulders.

"Hey, Abby, you know Perkins Drive-In is still open. Why don't we get somethin' to eat?"

"Sounds great," she said. "Is it okay if we eat it down at the lake?" God, this girl is a dream, he thought.

When they arrived at the lake, he grabbed two blankets from the trunk, one for the ground and another for her. They sat under the full moon eating burgers and sipping hot coffee.

"So why are you going all the way to Nebraska?" she asked.

"Twin Peaks doesn't have much to offer," he said. "I've never been much of a student… not like you. But this college is willin' to take me, and besides, I got family there. Lived with them one summer when I was a kid and haven't seen 'em since. They offered me a place to stay until I can find somethin' of my own."

"What about you—why California?"

"Same reasons," she answered. "My Grandma Hazel has a great house near the beach, and there's a good school there where I can study to become a nurse."

"You'd be great at it," he said.

She smiled at him and asked, "Mr. Riley, how do you know that?"

"Because I can read people," Jim answered. "Always been able to— kind of a gift I have. Want to know what I see in you?"

She looked at him, wide-eyed and said nothing.

"You're the most special person I have ever known," he said softly.

She felt her eyes begin to mist over as he reached for her hand. "Abby, I know that right now I have nothing to offer you, but can we please see each other again? Don't know about the future, I just want you in my life now to share as many todays as we have." He then pulled her close and kissed her tenderly as the lights of Twin Peaks twinkled in the distance.

When she arrived home, Gretchen was waiting in the living room. Her daughter was beaming, and for that she was grateful.

"Well, how was it?" she asked.

"Mama, I think I'm in love" was Abby's reply as she headed upstairs for bed.

Thirteen

George and Carla had left the dance at ten p.m. He had sensed that Jim was uncomfortable with his latest fling, so they had gone back to his house as the rest of the family was away for the weekend. They had opened the liquor cabinet and proceeded to down several shots of Tequila before making their way to the bedroom.

He awakened on Sunday to find Carla gone and stumbled downstairs to make some breakfast. His head was pounding when the phone rang. "Hey buddy," his friend asked, "isn't Abby terrific?"

"Yeah, great," George replied. "How was she?"

Jim knew what he meant, and replied, "We went out to the lake, watched the moon, and I drove her home."

George paused for a moment, thinking his friend had taken leave of his senses and said, "That's it?"

"I told you before," Jim replied, "she's different from the others."

"Yeah she must be," replied George. "Never thought Jimmy Riley would come home from bein' with a gorgeous dame without scorin'. What are ya doin' today?"

"Thought I'd go down to the diner and order breakfast. Abby starts work at eleven," Jim said.

"Geez, you just saw her last night," George replied. "How 'bout we go swimmin' at the hot springs pool? I'm ready to meet a new gal. That Carla was a firecracker in the sheets, but you know I can't keep it to just one at a time, buddy."

His friend paused and said, "Not today, I'll see you tomorrow at school."

When Jim hung up, George knew that something had changed between them and felt an overwhelming sense of loss.

Abby rose early the next morning and leashed up their sheepdog, Barkley, for a morning walk. Got lots to think about, she reflected. As they strode through the neighborhood, she welcomed the quiet solitude of the morning. Being with Jim had been better than imagined, but what now? Weren't they both going their separate ways in a few months? Why get into a relationship that had no future? She had always followed her own expectations and done what was sensible. She had her life planned… at least up until last night. She would get her degree, secure a position at a reputable hospital, marry a man that loved her, and was as equally focused as she was.

Jim Riley did not fit that mold…yes, he was going to business school in Nebraska, but she knew that he would be playing the field while he was there. He was not to be tied down, at least not yet, she thought. He could dazzle her all he wanted, but to pursue anything beyond last night was a road leading nowhere. But there was that voice in her head that said, "I think I'm in love." Now, what am I to do about that?

"I need to talk to Mama," she said to herself and proceeded on her way back home.

Gretchen had just started breakfast when her daughter came through the door and said, "Coffee?"

"Thanks, Mama," she replied. "Got a minute?" Abby asked.

"Really think you're in love, huh?" her mother asked.

"I'm confused," said Abby. "I had everything all planned out, and then he comes along."

Gretchen chuckled and said, "That's the way it usually happens dear, when you're least expecting it. Question is, what now?"

"I'm leaning towards telling him what a great night it was, and let's leave it at that," Abby replied.

Gretchen looked intently at her daughter. "That's what your head

says… how about your heart?" her mother asked.

"I know he could break it if I open myself up to him," Abby replied. "Is it worth the risk, Mama?"

"That's a question you'll have to answer for yourself." We can talk some more later when you get home from work. I need to leave for church now."

After her mother left, Abby sat in the kitchen sipping coffee, pondering the realization that her world had just been shaken.

Jim took a long bath in the tub and tried to think about how to approach Abby. He wanted to see her again, so much that he ached. Had he scared her off, talking about sharing just the present with her? He knew she had her future planned and maybe he wasn't right for her. Gotta give it a try, he thought. We can take it as far as we can, see what happens.

He took his time dressing in his favorite outfit, a gray zoot suit with black and white saddle oxfords. Bess was downstairs cooking breakfast for their guests. "Dressed up again?" she asked. "She must be somethin' special."

"She definitely is," he said, and headed down the street to the diner.

UNTIL WE MEET *Again*

Fourteen

The Hopkins Diner was located in downtown Twin Peaks on a corner lot in the middle of Main Street. The interior was lined with red vinyl booths facing the street. There were also ten tables and a counter with the same décor. It served good, old-fashioned American fare, and, in spite of the war, the business had remained steady, visited often by 'the regulars.' Tom was the second-generation owner, as Tom Sr. had opened the restaurant in 1930 and had passed away last year. His wife, Beth, had gone to live with her sister in Boise, and Tom Jr. had grown up helping his parents run the place.

This particular April Sunday morning found him in the kitchen frying bacon and eggs, as the cook had called in sick. He had just finished the order when Abby arrived. Although he knew she had gone to the dance the night before with Jim Riley, he was reluctant to press her for information. I'll let her tell me herself, he thought. She had worked for him three months now, and he looked forward to the smiling face that had become part of his life twenty hours a week. The customers had taken a shine to her, too, and he knew she had helped grow the business as some came to eat only when she was working. She was leaving soon, and he was already feeling a sense of loss.

Sixteen years ago, he had been engaged to Vivian Mays, and loved her deeply. They were sitting at the diner discussing wedding plans while on their lunch break.

"What do you think about September" she asked him. "Fall weddings can be beautiful, and we could use some of the autumn colors for the flowers and decorations. The girls would look great with darker dresses…it would accentuate their hair and skin tones. What do you think, Tom?"

"Honey, you're the expert in that department," he replied. Not that he

UNTIL WE MEET *Again*

wanted to be left out of the plans. He just knew that with her sense of style and class, their wedding day would be beautiful, and he trusted her completely.

As they enjoyed their apple pie, he caught her admiring the engagement ring. When he proposed and she opened the little box, he knew he'd picked a winner. It was a one-carat, almost flawless marquis diamond in a platinum setting. Nothing was too good for his girl, and he didn't care if it had taken a chunk from his savings.

He had been exempted from the war due to a partial hearing loss in his right ear from childhood infections. He had left Twin Peaks to obtain a business degree from the University of Idaho and four years later returned and accepted a banking officer position at the local Bank of America. He was now twenty-six years old and had managed to invest wisely, even bought a few rental properties. Yes, he was a lucky man and couldn't wait to share his life with Vivian. She had worked at Wilson's Furniture for six years and, with hard work, became their top design consultant.

After they were married, she had decided to vacate her apartment, become a homemaker, and the couple would move into Tom's rental property on Maple Street. It was a charming three-bedroom home with a big front porch, white picket fence, and a large back yard.

"Great house to start a family in," they had said.

"Needs a woman's touch, dear," she'd commented when he had first shown it to her. "I love it…we're going to be so happy here, aren't we?"

The current tenant was moving out in August, so a September wedding would be perfect for them. They had just finished their pie and coffee, when Vivian glanced down at her watch and said, "Dear God, where has the time gone?" I've got to dash, love. Got a one o'clock appointment with a client at the store. Could be a big purchase."

He stood up to kiss her goodbye and said, "I'll be by right after work to pick you up, okay? I promised dad I'd sit here and have a cup of coffee with

him." He sat back down and a few moments later noticed that Tom Sr. was standing behind the counter with a shocked look on his face. "Tommy, better go outside," and Tom instantly knew something horrible had just happened. He ran out onto the sidewalk and saw Vivian lying face down in the street, covered in blood.

"I didn't have time to stop, honest mister," the driver said. "She wasn't lookin' and just stepped right in front of my truck."

By now, a small crowd had gathered, waiting for the ambulance to arrive. He held her in his arms until it arrived and rode with them to the hospital.

As he waited in the hallway, family and friends rallied around. After two hours, he saw the doctor walking down the long corridor, still in his surgical gown. It was spotted with red, and his demeanor told Tom that he was about to receive the worst news of his life.

"How's my Viv?" he asked. "A real trooper, isn't she?"

The doctor looked drawn as he mustered up the words. "Son," he said, "we tried everything possible…just too many injuries, too much blood loss. I'm so sorry."

Tom stood there in shock as their loved ones cried and tried to console him. But it didn't work, and he wanted to be alone with his pain. He thanked them for coming, got in his car and drove to Hannigan's Bar, where he drank himself into oblivion.

During the years that followed, he had dated a few women, but had never had a serious relationship since her death. In many ways, Abby reminded him of Vivian—warm, kind, friendly…and beautiful. As he continued cooking that morning, he realized how much he would miss her, but knew that her dreams were larger than Twin Peaks. Hopefully, she'll come home often to visit, he thought.

And, for the first time since losing Vivian, Tom Hopkins wished he were twenty-six years old again.

Fifteen

Jim entered the diner and saw Abby back in the kitchen helping Tom with an order. He sat down at the counter and put a menu up to cover his face. When she walked by and glanced over, he slowly slid it down to reveal the boyish grin. Try as she might, a chuckle escaped before she could catch it.

"Gotcha laughin' already," he said.

"Is that what life's all about… one big joke?" she asked, trying to keep up the pretense of being on guard.

"Hey cut me some slack, I'm only seventeen, at least for one more day. How about celebratin' my birthday with me tomorrow?"

"I had no idea that last night I went out with a younger man," she replied.

"How old are ya?" Jim asked.

"Turned eighteen in February," she said.

He looked at her intently and said, "Abby, are you tryin' to say you won't go out with me anymore because you're two months older?" he asked, grinning. Abby knew that reason wasn't valid, and quite frankly, she wanted to say yes anyway.

"What'd you have in mind?" she asked.

"Well," he said, "there's this great nightclub in Livingston. You know, Big Band, all that. Tommy Dorsey's playin' there tomorrow night. How 'bout it?"

"Are you planning on getting drunk?" she asked.

"Maybe just one or two," he said.

She looked at him and realized that all her defenses were down and said, "It's a school night, and doesn't make any sense to go…but it is your birthday, and I wouldn't want you to celebrate it by yourself. Okay, I'll go, but I gotta be home by midnight."

"Now, Abby, what will your folks say?" he asked with a twinkle in his eye.

"You leave that to me," she replied. "And I'll be the one driving us home."

On Monday morning, George stopped by to drive his best friend to school as he had done everyday for the past three years. "Happy Birthday, buddy," he said. "Got the whole evenin' planned. Right after school, we'll go over to the pool hall and I'll let you win…ya know, it's your birthday and all." You don't wanna go?" he said noticing the reaction on Jim's face.

"George, can you pull the car over?" Jim asked. At that moment, his friend knew that the evening was not going to be as he had planned. "I asked Abby out again, and she said yes."

Feeling displaced, George quickly responded with "Okay, we'll pick up the girls and go together."

Jim looked at him soulfully and said, "We made plans to be alone."

George was hurt, but tried to mask it and said, "We been together on every birthday since we were kids. Guess things are changin'. Better check with you first from now on before I make any plans."

"It's just that I have a short time to get to know her," Jim said. "We're both leavin' Twin Peaks after the summer's over and I might not ever see her again."

George re-started the engine, glanced at his friend, and said nothing at all.

Abby had arranged to meet Jim at his house for their second date. She had told Gretchen that it was his birthday and they would be home by midnight. She had omitted the fact that they were going to a nightclub, and that her date would be drinking. Abby was grateful that her mother hadn't asked any more questions. She didn't like withholding things from Gretchen

as she had always been her rock, the one she trusted most in her life.

Jim was sitting on the front porch when Abby drove up. "Let's take my folks' car… I want to drive us there, and you can drive home, how's that?" he asked.

As they settled in, she asked, "Where's this place you're taking me?" "Just off the Interstate about a mile," he answered. "For now, just relax, sit back, and enjoy the radio." At that moment, soft romantic music began playing and he slipped his arm around her shoulder. She nestled down toward him and they drove the rest of the way in silence.

When they arrived, she was surprised at the size of the Club. It was a large ballroom lined with a wooden dance floor. The band had not yet started to play, and Jim found them a table near the front of the stage.

"What can I get for you?" he asked.

"I'll have a cherry coke," she replied. He re-appeared quickly with her drink and a beer for himself. "Abby, I'm not real good with words, but it means a lot to me, havin' you here on my birthday."

She looked at him and knew at once that he truly meant it. "Thanks for asking me," she said.

The band began filing in, and she noticed that he darted up to the stage. He quickly returned and said, "I want to dance the first one with you."

As she stood up to take his hand they danced to *Until We Meet Again*, and for the two of them, the rest of the evening was as magical as their first one.

Sixteen

During the next four months, Jim and Abby were inseparable, and both content to be so. After graduation, Jim took a job as a grocery clerk at the Food Fair Market just down the street from Hopkins Diner. He and Abby would often have lunch together, and she found herself adapting to his quick Irish wit.

"Sure and be'goura, those be some interestin' dents you have at the top o' your ears, Jimmy Riley," she said in her best Irish accent, as she pinched the top of his right ear.

"Well, Abbs," he replied, "these dents been in the family nigh on to a hundred years—wondered how long it'd be 'fore you noticed 'em!"

He'd taken to calling her Abbs when they were joking around. But, when being serious, it was always Abby. She had begun calling him Jimmy and noticed that he liked it…must sound less formal, she'd thought.

It was the first week of August, and Friday was their last night together. On Saturday morning, she was flying to California to live with Grams, and Jim knew that nothing he could say would change her mind. When she came home from work on Thursday, Gretchen told her that he had stopped by to talk with her.

Abby reflected back on all they had shared these past months and knew that saying goodbye was going to be the hardest thing she had ever done. She knew that he cared for her, but he was still too emotionally immature for a long-term commitment. And then, there were her goals, her dream. In two years, with study and hard work, she envisioned herself in the white uniform, helping her patients and soothing their pain.

Sometimes her thoughts transcended to a future when Jimmy would knock at her door, ready to settle down, and they would build a life together. And, then again, he could likely go off to Nebraska and take up with one doll after another she thought. Well, one thing she knew for sure, Abby Lansing was not the kind of girl that would try to lasso a man who didn't want to be tied down. That would only bring misery to them both and kill off everything they had meant to each other. But she knew that whatever happened on their last night together would always be part of her, and Jimmy Riley would forever hold a special place in her heart.

It was seven o'clock when the doorbell rang. He had arrived with a bouquet of yellow roses wearing a neatly ironed shirt and pants. His hair was perfectly coiffed, and the cool night breeze wafted his after-shave through the screen door.

"Abby, tomorrow's our last night together. Wondered if you wanted to go down by the lake, take a picnic supper, watch the sunset. Full moon too, just like our first date."

She always marveled at how he remembered every detail of their time shared together. "I have to work until six. Can you pick me up then?"

"You got it," he said.

She opened the door and stepped outside.

"These are for you," he said, handing her the flowers.

"They're beautiful. Thanks, Jimmy," she said as her eyes filled with tears…see you tomorrow."

They kissed, and she stood on the porch waving goodbye and watched him drive away.

At five o'clock the next day, Abby was wondering where all the customers were. There had always been an early dinner crowd that starting arriving by now. It was Friday, their popular Fish 'n Chips night, and customers were usually lined out the door by five-thirty. "Where is everyone?" she'd asked Tom. "Oh, they'll be here," he replied.

Little did she know that Jim and Tom had collaborated on a surprise going away party for her and about one hundred people were expected. The guests were to gather down the street in the parking lot of the Merc and all arrive together.

She had just gone into the restroom to primp a little before Jimmy arrived. When she walked back into the diner, everyone yelled, "Surprise!" She glanced around to find a sea of familiar faces—customers, friends, and family. And at the forefront was Jimmy, looking as though he had already had a beer or two. She ran over and hugged him in a way that made him never want to leave this place in time.

"We're all here to say goodbye and good luck to the most beautiful girl in the world," he said to everyone in the diner. Tom had prepared a special feast for everyone, and the guests stuffed themselves on fried chicken, mashed potatoes, sautéed fresh summer squash, corn bread, and homemade apple pie topped with ice cream for dessert.

When everyone had finally gone, Abby asked "Tom, do you want us to help you clean up?"

He approached her with tears and said, "What I want is for you to make your dream come true. And don't forget all of us who love you."

He kissed her cheek and once more experienced the pain of someone precious leaving his life.

Seventeen

They arrived at the lake just as the sun was setting. As he had done that first night back in April, Jim spread a blanket on the ground, and they sat facing the mountains.

"Lovely evening," Abby remarked.

"Hey Abbs, ever play craps?" he asked.

"Oh sure," she replied. "I hang out in gambling halls everyday."

"Got some dice here—wanna learn?" he asked.

She knew that he was not yet ready to be serious about this being their last night together. "Sure, why not?" she replied and for the next hour they laughed as always.

As the dusk vanished, a slight breeze blew up from the canyon. "Never was a boy scout, but I'm still prepared," he said as he opened the trunk of the car and brought out an ax, firewood, and an extra blanket.

As he stripped off his shirt, she once again admired his lean, muscular physique. She had seen it before as they had come here several times to swim in the lake, but had never seen his body silhouetted in the impending darkness. A slight chill come across her body and for a brief moment, her mind raced over the past four months, all they had shared, all that he meant to her.

He continued chopping the wood and then started the fire with kindling and newspaper. "Are you warm enough? he asked as the fire glistened.

She nodded, and he asked, "Abby, will you dance with me?" The full moon had just started to rise over the top of the mountains and there wasn't a cloud in the sky.

"Just wait right here." He returned bearing an old Victrola record player and a moment later they were dancing once more to *Until We Meet Again.* She knew what was about to happen and had to admit that she had come here to give herself to him. What lay ahead for them in the future was unknown, but for now, for this moment in the moonlight, their world was the lake, the firelight and the passion they both wanted to share.

When the music ended, neither of them spoke. He took her hand and gently guided her to the blanket. They lay down and he tenderly kissed her lips. She could feel her heart racing as he slowly unbuttoned her blouse. When his hands touched her breasts for the first time, it made her gasp, and when his lips found them, she moaned with pleasure. She held him tight, kissing the back of his neck, pulling him on top of her. For a moment, he paused and looked deeply into her eyes.

He was naked now, and her hands stroked his chest. She could feel his heart pounding, feel his manhood. Her hands began stroking him there… amazed that it felt natural and right to be doing so. She slowly removed her clothing and, as he entered her, she was catapulted into an ecstasy she had never known. When he exploded inside her body, she climaxed in waves and hoped it would never end.

Jimmy covered her up and they lay in the fire's glow for a while. He then rolled over, propped himself up on one arm, looked down at her and said. "Abby, you know I'm not ready for anything more than what we have right now. I can't settle down, not yet."

She hesitated for a moment, searching for the right words. "Jimmy, don't you think I know that? And my dream hasn't changed just because we made love tonight. Let's just leave it like this for now."

He put his arms around her once again, felt his tears begin to fall and heard her softly weeping. They lay there until after midnight holding each other tenderly.

"We'd better go Jimmy," she said reluctantly. "I have a long day ahead

of me tomorrow." He slowly packed up the car, and she slid over next to him, laying her head on his shoulder.

They arrived at her house and sat there quietly for a moment. "Well, I guess this is it," he said. You'll always be the most beautiful girl in the world to me…I'll never forget you, Abby. Not ever!"

He kissed her hand, and after doing so said, "Until we meet again."

She gently brushed back his hair while saying, "I'll miss you Jimmy, more than you know."

Then she opened the car door and walked out of his life.

Eighteen

The Twin Peaks Airport was quiet when the Lansing family arrived. It was Abby's first flight, and she was thankful that they were not having any summer thunderstorms that morning. They stood together in the small terminal until it was time for her to board.

"Don't cry Cora," she told her little sister. "Aren't you excited to be finally getting your own room?" Abby asked.

"Not if it means you have to leave us," Cora replied, sniffling.

"I'm not leaving forever. I'll be back at Thanksgiving, remember?"

Abby kissed her cheek, then hugged and kissed the rest of her family. She was surprised at how emotional Kenneth was at her leaving. "Study hard, little girl," he said, choking back tears. Gretchen was doing her best not to break down.

"We're so proud of you honey. Give Grams a big kiss from me, okay?"

"I will, Mama," Abby promised as she bent down to grab her luggage.

She walked out onto the tarmac and looked up to find them all waving at the window. She waved back and walked up the steps to the plane. When she had settled in, her thoughts drifted to Jimmy, and she knew that he would always be a part of her, that she would never forget him, and deeply wanted him in her life again someday.

Abby arrived at the San Francisco Airport at noon. Hazel was waiting for her inside the terminal, and when she spotted her granddaughter, her face lit up in a way Abby had never seen before. After exchanging hugs, they began their drive down to Santa Cruz. "How far is it, Grams?" Abby asked.

"Oh, 'bout ninety minutes…we'll be there before you know it. You've never seen the ocean, and I am so excited that you're here!"

Her grandmother noticed that she looked different, more a woman than a girl. "How's that young man of yours?" she asked.

Abby then related to her the events of the past four months, and that she would always care for Jimmy. She did not discuss their last night together, as she didn't want to share that with anyone else. That was intimate, special, just between the two of them.

"Sounds like you had quite a summer," Hazel said. She sensed that there was more to Abby's story, but didn't want to pry. After all, they hadn't seen each other since last Christmas and had some catching up to do. And she realized that this was a big step for her granddaughter...leaving her home, her family, and all that was familiar.

"Once we get home, why don't we put on our suits and go down to the beach for a swim?" Hazel asked.

She noticed the excitement on Abby's face and continued, "When I left home this morning, it was a beautiful, sunny day. Sometimes during the summer we get fog, but today's spose to be about eighty degrees."

"You swim in the ocean, Grams?" Abby asked wideyed. "I never knew you did that—it's not too cold for you?"

"Well, it took a while, but I'm used to it now," Hazel replied. "When I was taking care of Genevieve, she put the bug in my ear to try it. and sometimes she and I go together. Another thing I started doing was fishing. See there's this old cement ship down at Seacliff Beach in Aptos. It used to be a big dance hall fifteen years ago. and now people just walk out on the deck and fish off the pier of the ship. Mostly catch perch. Sometimes I go there just to watch the marine life...otters, sea lions, pelicans, dolphins. There's a great walking path along the beach too. I think you're really going to love it here, honey!"

Abby looked at her grandmother for a moment and realized that she continued to be amazing. I want to be just like her, she thought.

When they pulled in the driveway, Abby noticed how different the

landscape was from her neighborhood in Twin Peaks. Gram's street was lined with eucalyptus and large cypress trees. She stepped out of the car and felt the balmy ocean breeze caress her face. The lawns were beautifully manicured, and in the distance she could hear the sound of shorebirds. Grams was right, she thought—I am going to love it here. If only Jimmy could see this.

"Over here honey," Hazel said. "Welcome to your new home."

Grams owned a two-story home that had a large kitchen and living room, three bedrooms, two baths, a covered patio, and two upstairs balconies with ocean views.

"Your room is on the second floor," Hazel said.

As they went up the stairs, Abby noticed there were some beautiful watercolor paintings hung on the walls.

"That's something else I've taken up since I moved here," she said. They were exquisite seascapes and once again, Abby marveled at her grandmother's many talents.

When she opened the door, her eyes filled with tears. "Grams, you remembered," she cried.

Hazel hugged her and said, "You didn't think I'd forget your favorite colors, did you?" Her grandmother had painted and decorated the room in lavender with crème accents. There was a double bed covered in a beautifully quilted spread, with lovely floral throw pillows. Across the room was a painted rocker, draped with a lavender throw. Next to it was a lovely desk and chair, which were placed in front of the french doors. Abby opened them and went out onto the balcony.

The view was breathtaking as she inhaled the rich ocean air and could see several families enjoying themselves on the beach. Hazel stepped out to join her and couldn't remember a time when she had seen Abby so overcome with emotion.

"There's one more thing I want you to have," she said and held up a beautiful painting that would perfectly adorn her granddaughter's room.

"Where would you like to hang it?" she asked.

"I love you Grams. Thanks….for everything."

Nineteen

Virgil Hobbs had moved twenty miles to Santa Cruz from San Jose three years ago after serving four years in the Army Air Corps as a bomber pilot in the South Pacific. He loved the small ocean town and had spent summer vacations in the area at the family's beach home. He had begun doing small remodeling jobs prior to getting a general contractor's license—his business was built on referrals and a strong work ethic. Sometimes it was all he could do to handle the workload without having to take on a hired hand. He wanted to continue on his own for as long as possible, he'd thought; that way, I know it'll be done right. Early on, he'd been hired as a subcontractor and had seen first hand the shoddy work that some in the trades had done. That had been the main motivation to start his own business, and after three years, he was well known in the community as a custom carpenter and master craftsman.

Even though he could now afford to own a larger home, he was happy with his bungalow overlooking the beach. He had completely remodeled the inside with cherry wood cabinetry, new tile countertops, and hardwood floors. In the upstairs bath, he had installed a beautiful sunken tub surrounded with block glass. He had paneled the walls half-way up with bead board and topped it with wainscoting. The floors were marble, and he had hired an interior designer to consult on the paint color and add the finishing touches. He had put so much of himself into the place and felt attached to it. Besides, there was easy access to surfing, his favorite hobby. Unless he had to be at a job site in the early morning, he would rise, grab his surfboard, and head down to the ocean. About seven o'clock, he'd head back home to shower, have breakfast, and leave for work.

He was just pulling into his garage when he spotted his neighbor, Hazel Barrymore, who lived next door. He had never before seen the young lady that was with her…wonder if this is the granddaughter she's always bragging about, he thought.

Hazel spotted him immediately, waved, and smiled. "Virgil, I'd like you to meet my granddaughter, Abby."

He stood there for a moment, captivated by her beauty. "Nice to meet you," he said, almost stammering. "Your Grandma wasn't exaggerating," and Abby felt herself blush.

"Virgil's one of the best carpenters in this town," Hazel chimed in. "Not only that, he's a great neighbor…helped me fix things more times than I can count."

Abby studied him for a moment and said, "Sounds like you're a handy person to have around. Thanks for helping Grams. Well, we better go start dinner. Nice meeting you, Virgil."

After they went inside, he felt as though he had just been struck by a thunderbolt.

During breakfast the next morning, Hazel had given Abby the directions to the college. "Registration starts today," she'd said. "With your grades, there shouldn't be any problem getting into the program. Genevieve and I are spending the day shopping for her a new car, so I probably won't be home until early evening. Oh, and speaking of cars, why don't you come on out to the garage for a minute."

That was the only room Abby hadn't seen yet, and she wondered how many more surprises Grams had in store for her. It was draped with heavy canvas, and when Hazel removed it, underneath was a yellow, 1938 Chevrolet convertible.

Abby gasped and stood there in disbelief. "Where did you get it?" she asked, noticing the twinkle in her grandmother's eye.

"Got it for a song," she answered. "It was a junker, and Virgil helped

me restore it."

Geez, is there anything that guy can't do? she thought.

"It's for you to enjoy, honey. After all, what's the fun of living at the beach without a convertible to drive?"

Abby slid into the crème colored leather upholstery and almost felt the urge to pinch herself. "Grams, I don't believe I deserve all this," Abby said.

"Are you kidding?" replied Hazel. "You are one of the most special people God ever put on this earth. Some day, young lady, I hope you do believe it."

She then opened the garage door and watched her granddaughter drive away, her beautiful auburn hair blowing in the cool breeze of the morning.

Twenty

It was Monday morning, and Jim was walking to work, thinking only of Abby. Hell, it's all I have thought about since she left, he concluded. He knew it wouldn't be easy letting her go, but he had no idea how much a part of his life she'd become until she had actually gone. When he had these thoughts, his mind would drift to the place of total commitment and what that implied.

He couldn't imagine loving even Abby that much…to never be with another woman again, as long as he lived. Going to work each day and coming home to the same person every night. And God, what if she got pregnant? He had never felt love from his own parents, so how could he even begin to know how to love a child and be a good father? History would probably repeat itself, and I'd make a mess of the whole deal, hurting her in the process, he thought. They had never said "I love you" to each other. So why did his insides ache at the very thought of her?

He looked around and saw George pulled up at the curb. "Hey buddy, we're only gonna be in town 'til Saturday. Let's start celebratin', okay?"

"Oh, so you've decided to go with me to Nebraska after all," Jim said.

"Heck yeah," George quipped, "and I got it all arranged. My old man's givin' us enough money to stop at a couple of hotels 'til we get there, and he covered our first three months, so we won't need to stay with your relatives out there. I tell ya, my friend, right now it's time for the two of us to pick up where we left off."

Jim knew exactly what was meant by that…time to start in again with the girls, the drinkin'.

"Sure George," he said. "What'd you have in mind for tonight?"

"There's this new dame in town, Jimmy. Name's Dottie, heard she's a hottie." He was expecting a laugh on that one, and got only a slight grin instead. "What's the matter with you, man?" asked George. "That Lansing doll has got you all twisted up in your head. Just let her go."

If only it were that easy, thought Jim. "Why don't you swing by and pick me up about seven, okay George?" He then went inside, feeling more emptiness than he had ever felt before.

George was honking as Jim walked out to the car. "Carla and Dottie are meetin' us at Joe's," said George. It was one of the local saloons in town, a step down from Hannigan's. It had pool tables and Jim suspected that George had chosen it so that his friend could "break the ice" with Dottie over a game of pool. When they arrived, the two girls were seated at a table in the bar area, waiting for their dates to arrive and buy them their first drink of the evening.

"Hi, I'm Dottie," she said and reached out to shake his hand. He had to admit that she was attractive, blond wavy hair, blue eyes, delicate facial features, good figure.

"Jim," he said, extending his hand, "Jim Riley."

The guys ordered drinks and they let the girls rack the balls.

"Let's play girls against the guys," Carla suggested.

During the game, Jim suspected that his friend was purposely letting them win. He took him aside and said, "What are you doing?"

"Simple buddy," George replied with a grin. "Don't you want Dottie in the best mood possible? Your chance of scorin' tonight will definitely go up if she is, my friend."

Jim had already suspected the motive before George had said it. They continued playing, and he gave in to letting the girls win. More drinks were ordered, and they left the place about nine.

Once they got in George's car, Jim glanced over at Dottie. They were in the back seat, and this is where the former Jim Riley would already be making his move. She turned to find him staring at her, when George said, "Hey everybody, it's a full moon. Let's drive up to the lake."

Jim suddenly felt his heart pound….wasn't it just three nights ago that he had shared that wonderful evening with Abby? Wonder what she's doing right now, at this very moment, he thought.

"Are you okay?" Dottie asked, looking worried.

"Yeah, fine, just fine," he said. But he knew that he was as far from fine as a person could be.

They arrived at the lake just before dark and got out of the car. George and Carla went off by themselves, leaving Jim alone with Dottie.

"You don't really want to be here with me, do you?" she asked him.

"Dottie, look…it's not that I don't think you're pretty and all…I do."

"You're hung up on another girl aren't you?" she asked.

"Is it that obvious?" he replied.

"Well," she answered, "the word on the street is that Jim Riley is a womanizer. If you weren't missin' someone else, we'd be doin' what they're doin' right now," she said and glanced over in the direction where George and Carla had gone.

"Guess I'm not a very good date, am I?" he asked.

"Don't worry," she said. "I know what it's like to have someone get under your skin like that. I won't say a word, promise."

He lit them both a cigarette and they stood there watching the moonrise. When George and Carla returned, they all got back in the car. When they reached his home, Jim thanked Dottie for the evening and went inside upstairs to his room.

He thought again of Abby and remembered the smell of her hair, her skin, the feeling of her beneath him. God, when will this pain subside, when will I start living my life again?

It was at that moment Jim Riley realized he came to life the day he fell in love with Abby Lansing.

Twenty-One

Abby pulled into the large parking lot of Redwoods College that had received its name from the coastal redwood trees that were prominent in the area. It was located less than twenty miles from Big Basin Redwoods State Park, boasting trees some three hundred feet tall. Hazel had promised to take her there for a day hike on the weekend.

She found her way to the Admissions Office and registered for all the required courses, fifteen units in all. Yes, it was a heavy load, but with Gram's help, she didn't have to work. "Just study and reach your dream," she'd said. Abby walked the grounds of the campus, and, to her delight, it was much larger than she had imagined.

She was headed back out to the car and spotted Virgil backing out of a parking stall. "Taking the day off?" she asked him.

"Just the morning," he replied. "I signed up to take an evening Oceanography class. Planning on opening up my own Surf Shop some day. Well, guess I'll see you and Hazel tonight. She asked me over for dinner."

"Oh?" Abby said, surprised.

He sensed her hesitation and said, "Abby, if it's not a good time, we can take a rain check."

"No, it's fine," she replied. "Six o'clock?"

"Great, I'll be there," he said.

As he drove away, Abby couldn't help but think that Grams had some matchmaking up her sleeve. And at that moment, her thoughts once again drifted to Jimmy. Wonder if he's thinking of me too, she pondered as her car headed home.

She pulled into the garage and heard the phone ringing in the kitchen. "Listen honey," said Grams on the other line. "I had invited Virgil over for dinner tonight to thank him for helping me restore the car. Could you please just get it started? Everything's there, and he loves Italian. Homemade sauce and stuff for salad is in the fridge and pasta's in the cupboard. If you could just run out and get some sourdough bread at the Piggly Wiggly, then we'll be all set."

"I'll take care of it Grams," Abby replied. She got back in the car and left the store with bread and a fresh bouquet of flowers. Better make the table look nice, she thought.

Virgil arrived promptly at six o'clock. "I forgot to ask Hazel if there was anything I could bring. Hope this is all right," he said as he handed Abby the most delectable looking cheesecake she had ever seen. "It's New York style. Wow, the table looks beautiful. Did you do all this?"

"Yeah," she replied. "Grams is out helping my aunt buy a new car. She should be home soon, but if not, we'll have to start without her. Can't keep manicotti waiting forever, you know." She caught him looking at her inquisitively.

"It smells wonderful," he said. "How much longer before it's ready?"

"Half an hour," said Abby.

"Great," he said. "Have you had a chance to walk on the beach yet?"

"No, just sunbathing yesterday," she replied.

"Well, how about right now?" he asked. "I'll go next door, get my sandals, and be right back."

As they headed onto the sand, Abby realized this was the first time she had ever walked on the beach, and she was doing it with an almost complete stranger. Yet as they walked, she couldn't help but notice how attractive he was. He had a tanned, rugged appeal. He was mature, sure of himself, and what he wanted in life. They conversed and as the sun began to set over the ocean, Abby knew why her grandmother loved living here.

"What time is it?" she asked him.

"Six-thirty," he replied. She hadn't realized that thirty minutes had gone by so quickly. He was easy to talk to, she thought. "We'd better head back," she said.

They arrived home to find the phone ringing. "Hey honey," said Grams. "Your Aunt Genevieve's new beau came into town today on business and he wants to take us out to dinner. She's wanted me to meet him for several weeks. Is Virgil there yet?"

"Yes, he is," replied Abby.

"Tell him I'm sorry I can't make it tonight, and I'll bring him over some of my pot roast next week. He loves that. I'll be home about eleven."

"Okay, Grams, tell Aunt Genevieve hi for me," and as she hung up the phone Abby couldn't help but think that her grandmother had planned this in advance. Well, why wouldn't she think that it was okay to play matchmaker? Abby thought. She has no idea of what happened between Jimmy and me.

"Is Hazel all right?" asked Virgil.

"Oh yeah, she just needs to take a rain check on tonight. Said she'll make it up to you next week."

They finished the evening getting to know each other a little better and had dessert on the patio. When he left, Abby went upstairs and stepped out onto the balcony. The almost full moon was reflecting on the ocean, causing it to shimmer. Jimmy would love this, she thought and the words of their song filled her soul…

"Until we meet again, with moonlight in the sky."

She finally went back inside, cleaned up the kitchen, and crawled into bed, wishing he were next to her right now.

Until We Meet *Again*

Twenty-Two

Tuesday, August 14th, Jim had just finished putting Mrs. Johnson's groceries into her car, when George drove up, wilding waving a newspaper.

"Damn good news, Jimmy" he said. "The Japs just surrendered and your worries are over, pal! Why ain't you jumpin' up and down….hell, the whole town's already celebratin.'"

Jim looked at him with sarcasm. "B e c a u s e," he said slowly. "That doesn't mean I can't still get drafted. I'm not 4F like you and home free, at least not yet."

"Come on," said George. "What time you get off work?"

"Six," Jim replied. Why?"

"'Cuz Hannigans is servin' up nickel beer, my friend."

"George, we're leavin' for college before daybreak on Friday," Jim said. I'm gonna go home and start packin'—have one on me," he said as he flipped him a nickel.

George stood there dumbfounded, half in, half out of the car. "Jimmy, when we leave on Friday, it'll be just like old times, right?"

"Sure George," said Jim. When he uttered those words, he knew he wasn't being totally honest and wondered if he would ever return to the day when honesty varied, depending on the situation. Yes, Abby had changed that, without his knowing it until now. Could he ever return to his former life and most of all, did he want to? Today, he thought, I have absolutely no clue.

Hazel awoke the next morning to find Abby down at the beach on a chair under an umbrella, reading one of her school textbooks. "Well," she said to her granddaughter, "I don't think it's going to take long for you to adjust to California. Everything go all right last night?"

Abby looked up and surmised that Grams was trying to suppress a smile. "Sure," Abby replied. "Did you plan that, Mrs. Barrymore?"

"Why dear, how can you even think such a thing?" Hazel replied. "Can I help it if your aunt's fella unexpectedly shows up and insists on taking us both out to dinner?"

Abby studied her a bit more and decided to change the subject. "Virgil is really nice and I enjoyed his company. I actually ran into him yesterday morning at school."

"Oh?" Hazel said.

"Yes," Abby continued, "He's taking a night class—wants to open up a surf shop someday."

"Well," Grams said, "I know that whatever Virgil Hobbs does in life, he'll be successful. He's one of the most driven folks I've ever known."

Abby thought of Virgil and how different he was from Jimmy. He must be happy the war's over, she thought. I wonder if our paths will cross in the future, where will it happen, how will we both react? She once again reflected on the last words he had said to her, "until we meet again."

"Two more weeks of sun and you'll be brown as a berry!" Hazel remarked, breaking Abby's thoughts. "Don't know how that's gonna look with your red hair."

"Not to worry Grams," Abby said. "I don't plan on lounging on the beach until school starts. I want to spend the next few days getting to know my way around. Virgil told me about the big amusement park just down the road and the amazing roller coaster."

"Giant Dipper," replied Hazel. "You've never been on one, have you?"

"No, and I'm not sure I want to," said Abby. "When was the last time you were on it?" she asked her grandmother.

"Just last month when your cousin Ron was out visiting Genevieve. We got an all day pass and were there 'til night and the entire park was lit up," said Hazel.

In her mind, Abby pictured the rides, all brightly illuminated with the ocean as their floor, and she couldn't wait to see it. "Grams," she said, "I know we planned to drive to Big Basin Redwoods on Saturday. Do you think we could go to the Boardwalk on Sunday?"

"Sure," replied her grandmother. "We are going to have so much fun while you're here, just wait and see."

Fun, Abby thought. Now Jimmy, he knew how to have fun.

Little did Abby know that on that very afternoon, Jim Riley's carefree world was about to end. He walked home from work and as he entered the living room, noticed a letter addressed to him from the Selective Service System. He opened it, his heart pounding. The gist of the letter was that he was to report to Fort Benning, Georgia for Army boot camp next week. God, he thought, this is gonna be rough on George. He's really been wantin' to leave Twin Peaks and live in a big city. Maybe he can go on ahead to Omaha without me. After all, his dad's payin' for him to get started back there.

His mother entered the room and to Jim's surprise, looked sad as she reached out her hand to read the letter. "Only good news is, the war's over," she said. "I know you had your heart set on that college. Maybe you can still do it when you get out."

"Sure, Ma," he replied. "I better go downtown and give George the news. Can I borrow the car?"

He went outside and sat on the front porch, trying to gather his thoughts before leaving. Maybe it's for the best, maybe the Army will make a man outta me. If that happens, maybe I can still make it work with Abby. Yeah, and maybe she'll belong to someone else by then, too. A girl that beautiful, still not married four years from now—how realistic is that?

He started the engine, drove downtown and parked in front of Hopkins Diner, remembering their first dinner together and how much he had made her laugh. And for the first time since Saturday, he put his head down on the steering wheel of the car and sobbed uncontrollably.

Twenty-Three

George Chandler drove into downtown Twin Peaks, and for the life of him, couldn't remember a time when he felt more alive. The streets were lined with revelers, and all the bars were offering discounted drinks to celebrate the war's end. As he made his way into Hannigan's, he noticed Carla sitting in a booth towards the back. He didn't recognize her date and immediately took a seat at the bar.

"Scotch on the rocks," he told the bartender. As he sipped his drink, he would occasionally glance her way and noticed that they seemed to be working up to a heated discussion.

A tap on the shoulder broke his observation, and he turned around to find Jim looking solemn and noticed that his eyes were red and swollen. "What the hell?" George asked. "Hey, doctor, can you bring him a round of what I'm havin'?" George studied his friend for a moment and said, "Jimmy, you gotta snap out of it buddy. We're about to have the time of our lives when we get to Omaha."

And suddenly, George noticed Carla running out of the bar. Her date slowly stood up and as he walked by, George stuck his foot out and tripped him. He stumbled to his feet and swung at George with a surprise left hook, and soon he, Jim, and several others were knee deep in a brawl. Carla's man of the evening was eventually knocked out by someone other than George, and he and Jim headed outside.

"When I said I hoped it would be like old times, I was talkin' about when we get to Omaha," said George. "Never thought it would happen here again-- we're back in the saddle, old buddy!"

Jim paused for a moment and said, "George, the only saddle I'll be in is the one takin' me to Georgia next week," and he then proceeded to give his friend the news. "You know, Mike Peyton has been sayin' all along that if one of us got called up, he'd fill in. I know it's not like we planned, but there's nothin' I can do about it."

George looked at him and said, "I'll ask him, Jimmy. I just need to get outta here, you know, experience the big beautiful world a little."

"Yeah I do know," replied his friend, and wished that Uncle Sam was sending him to California.

George and Mike left early Friday morning in the convertible, packed to the hilt with all their belongings. It was a beautiful clear morning, just before sun-up and Jim had driven over to George's house to say good-bye. As the last item was put in the car, he thrust out his hand and then threw both arms around George in a bear hug. The action took his friend aback—their circumstances had never forced the two of them into such emotion before.

George hugged him, too, and said, "Well, guess this is it for a while. Been a pleasure knowin' ya, Jimmy Riley."

"Hey buddy," replied Jim, "it's not like we're never gonna see each other again. I'll be done with boot camp in six weeks—maybe I can get a furlough and we could meet halfway."

"Sure," said George and even though both knew it probably wouldn't happen, it was all that either could say at the moment.

As George and Mike got into the car, Jim waved goodbye and had never felt more alone.

Twenty-Four

Abby spent the next few days driving the area in her yellow convertible, exploring the beauty of the central coast of California. On Friday, she had driven to Monterey and spent the day walking and having lunch on the pier. It was seventy-five degree weather, and as she sat outside the restaurant enjoying a bowl of fresh clam chowder, marveled at how different this was from Twin Peaks. She had phoned home last night and spoken with Gretchen. It was humid, and they were having one of the usual summer thunder and lightning storms.

She had just finished eating when she heard a familiar voice.

"Is this seat taken?" She looked up to find Virgil standing there, wearing flowered Bermuda shorts, a T-shirt, and sandals. "Didn't mean to startle you," he said with a little chuckle.

"Oh, you didn't," Abby replied, trying to keep her composure. "You're not working today?"

"I'm starting a large remodeling job on Monday, so I actually have a day to myself," he said. "Do you mind if I join you?"

"Please do," she answered and at that moment the waiter appeared and took his order.

"Would you like some dessert, Abby?" he asked.

"No thanks, gotta watch the figure," and as she said it, noticed that he looked at her admiringly. "Do you come here often?" she asked.

"About three or four times a year," he said. "I like to surf in different places, and there's some great hiking trails here too."

They continued conversing for the next hour, and Abby realized that she again felt comfortable and relaxed with him. "What are your plans for the rest of the day?" he asked. "If you don't have to head out right away, I have a sailboat docked over there—we could take her out for awhile."

"Well, there's a first time for everything," she replied. "Guess it's time to start getting my sea legs. What's the name of your boat?" she asked.

"*The Abigail,*" he said with a wink. "Always liked that name."

He paid the check, and as they walked toward the boat, reached down and took hold of her hand. For the first time since leaving home, she felt her heart lighten, and felt that for the present, she was meant to be here.

Abby began the nursing program at Redwoods College the last week of August. She and Virgil had spent every evening together since that day in Monterey. They went to the movies, had beach picnics, and Hazel had insisted that it was fine for them to go to the Boardwalk without her. "I've been there so many times," she'd said.

The two drove there after Virgil finished work and rode on every ride. As they stood in line for the Giant Dipper roller coaster, he sensed her apprehension. "You'll be just fine," he said as he put his arm around her shoulder and gave her a gentle hug. "Remember what you said before we went sailing—there's a first time for everything!"

"How long is that first drop?" she asked, biting her lower lip.

"Oh, 'bout seventy-five feet. Don't worry, I'll be right here next to you. If they can do it, so can you," Virgil said as he pointed up ahead to a couple of children who appeared to be about ten years of age.

When they boarded and were secured in the ride, he reached over and held her hand. "Here we go," he said as the car slowly made its way up the long track.

They both screamed excitedly during the entire ride. and when it was over, she turned to him and said, "Thanks for making me do it. Can we go again?" she asked with a twinkle in her eye. He laughed, and they made their way around to get in line again.

They had dinner as the sun set on the ocean, and both ate corn dogs

laden with mustard, and later shared some cotton candy. When the park closed, they returned to Abby's car as Virgil had asked earlier if they could take the convertible. She wasn't sure why, and as they approached the Chevy, she asked "You want to drive? After all, you do have a vested interest in this car."

He chuckled and said, "Hazel and I had so much fun restoring it. She really wanted to make it nice for you."

"Thanks for helping her," Abby said. "I'm hoping that she'll let me buy it once I finish school and start working. Already attached to it, you know. Where did you want to go tonight?" she asked as he started the engine.

"There's a drive-in movie theatre in Santa Cruz, and there's a great flick playing there tonight. Thought we could put the top down and watch it."

"That sounds great," she said, and realized it was why he had asked her to put two blankets in the trunk before they left the house.

As they drove she knew that with school starting next week they would be spending less time together. The counselor for the program had told her there would be a minimum of four hours of homework each evening. She glanced over at him and realized how much she had come to enjoy his company. When they parked, he opened the trunk and returned with the blankets.

Was it just two weeks ago that Jimmy had done this very thing, she asked herself? For a moment, Abby remembered that night, laying with him under the stars, and wondered if she would ever feel such passion again. Virgil then covered her snugly and kissed her gently on the cheek. Maybe I will, she thought, maybe I will.

Twenty-Five

Jim Riley boarded the train for Fort Benning, Georgia, the third week of August. He would be in boot camp for six weeks and then be transferred to a different post. The training was rigorous, and all the more difficult for him due to the extremely high humidity. In Twin Peaks, they would have occasional summer thunderstorms, but he had never experienced this kind of weather. The drill sergeant had instructed them all to take salt tablets to avoid dehydration, and he awoke one morning to find fungus growing in his army boots. What amazed him was how easily he adapted to the military. He had anticipated there would be problems adjusting, but found that he welcomed the disciplined regimen. Maybe they will make a man outta me after all, he thought.

He would then drift to thinking of Abby and had come to face the fact that she may never again be part of his life. He had resolved to try and reach her when boot camp was over and he had been re-assigned, just to say hello, see how she was doing, and secretly hoped they may someday have a future together. If she said the words "I've missed you," he knew he would take his first furlough and do everything possible to spend it with her. It was the one thought that sustained him over the next six weeks.

He applied himself, and, to his surprise, was promoted to E2 at the end of boot camp. But the biggest surprise was yet to come—he was being transferred to Ford Ord, California, located on the Central Coast, fifty miles from Santa Cruz. When Jim received the orders, he stood there dumfounded and couldn't believe his stroke of luck, couldn't believe he may be seeing her again this soon. "Will she feel as lucky as I do?" he wondered. Only one way to find out, as he headed back to the barracks to start packing.

Abby found the nursing program to be everything she had dreamed about. Yes, it was hard work, but she was no stranger to that. She had always been an excellent student, helped her mother with housework, taken care of her brother and sisters, and when she was old enough, worked part-time after school.

It was late September, and she and Virgil had been spending their free time together on the weekends. It was Saturday, and the two had planned another sailing adventure on his boat in Monterey. She was hurriedly getting ready to go and suddenly felt nauseous. Oh, God, hope I'm not getting the flu, she thought and barely made it to the bathroom before vomiting. She got up from the toilet, sat down on the bed and realized that over the past few days, she had felt queasy, especially in the morning. Until now, she had dismissed it as school jitters, adjusting to her heavy class load. She had also thought it might be that she often dashed out the door with little or no breakfast, much to Gram's dismay.

But as Abby continued reflecting over the past six weeks, she realized that for the first time ever, her period was late. The demands of her rigorous schedule had caused it to slip her mind and she suddenly felt chilled to the bone. No, this can't be—I can't be pregnant. What would I do? What would Mama and Grams think of me?

Just then the doorbell rang, and she knew it would be Virgil, ready to take her sailing. She had not told him about Jimmy, about the night they had shared together. As she went downstairs, she felt the need to tell Virgil everything, to be honest with him.

"Are you feeling okay, honey?" asked Grams. "You don't look too well."

"Abby, we can go sailing another time," said Virgil. "Are you up for a drive? Maybe we can just walk on the pier instead. There's something I want to talk to you about," he added.

"Sure," she replied, and then thought, "There's something I need to talk to you about, too."

Twenty-Six

Jim Riley arrived at Ford Ord a few days later and was amazed at the beauty of the area. It was eighty degrees without humidity, and he had never before seen the ocean. He had received a two-day leave and decided to take the bus into Monterey and spend the day on the pier. He had gotten Hazel's phone number when he arrived at the base, and his plan was to call Abby with the good news that he was stationed nearby and ask her to meet him today and have lunch.

He arrived at the pier about eleven o'clock in the morning and called Hazel. "Hello, Mrs. Barrymore. It's Jim Riley, a friend of Abby's. Is she there?"

Her grandmother was a bit surprised, and said, "No, actually, she's spending the day down at the pier in Monterey. Shall I give her a message?"

"No thanks," he stammered. "I'll call her later." And for the second time in a week, Jim Riley was in utter disbelief.

Virgil and Abby strolled hand in hand along the pier, found a bench and sat down. The drive down to Monterey had been a quiet one, and he sensed that something was troubling her. As they sat there, he leaned over and kissed her, then noticed that tears were slowly falling down her cheeks. "Oh, Virgil," she said. "I think I'm pregnant."

She expected him to act shocked, to look at her disapprovingly. Instead, he moved closer. "You want to talk about it?" he asked.

She told him about Jimmy, the time they had shared together, including the night at the lake, and that he wasn't ready yet to commit.

"I don't plan to tell him about this but God—what do I do now?"

"Abby, remember I said earlier I wanted to talk to you about something?" Well, I know we haven't known each other very long, but I've fallen in love with you." At that moment, he reached into his pocket and opened a box with a beautiful one-carat engagement ring.

"Abigail Lansing, will you marry me?"

"But what about the baby?" she asked. "That's a lot to take on, Virgil."

"If we get married soon, no one has to know that I'm not the baby's real father. Say yes, and you'll make me the happiest man in the world."

She looked intently at him and said, "Yes, I will marry you," and gently kissed him.

Jim Riley was seated at the window of a restaurant looking at the menu. He glanced out at the exact moment that Virgil slipped the ring on Abby's finger, saw her kiss him, and kept watching as they stood up to leave, holding hands. He looked away, felt his heart sink and the tears whelm up in his eyes. He walked back to the bus stop and returned to Ford Ord, trying to come to grips with fact that she was gone forever and there would never be another Abby as long as he lived.

Virgil and Abby were married the following week at a small ceremony on Twin Lakes Beach. Hazel had been ecstatic when she had learned that they were engaged, but puzzled when her granddaughter informed her that the wedding was to be the following weekend.

"Honey, no one has to tell me that Virgil's a great guy, but aren't you two rushing things a bit?"

Abby knew that she was acting out of character—after all, she had always been the one who planned, didn't rush into things, and she realized her recent behavior was unusual.

When she phoned Gretchen to give her the news, her mother paused on the other line, not responding. "Now, Mama, you know how much Grams thinks of Virgil," Abby said. "And you know he and I have been spending a lot of time together. He's a wonderful man, Mama, and he'll take good care of me, I just know it."

"But what about your school?" her mother asked.

"Nothing's changed," said Abby. "And besides, I'll be living right next door to Grams. Don't worry, okay? We'll fly out and spend Thanksgiving. You'll love Virgil, I promise."

"What about you, Abby, do you love him?" Her daughter paused a moment and said, "Mama, Virgil's here right now, and we're leaving to go pick out the wedding cake. I'll call you later, okay?"

She had just hung up the phone when Dr. Evans called to confirm that her pregnancy test was positive, and all Abby could think about was that she wanted her baby to have a good father. Even though she wasn't in love with Virgil, she cherished him for all that he was willing to do for them.

But down deep in her heart, she knew that she would never love him the same way as Jimmy Riley. Not ever.

UNTIL WE MEET *Again*

Twenty-Seven

Katie Rose Hobbs was born on May 8, 1946. She was small, weighing only 6 lbs., and was breech, so the birth had been difficult for Abby. She had a mop of red curls and blue eyes and, after the nurse finished bundling her, Virgil came in, beaming.

"She's beautiful," he said as his eyes filled with tears. Abby kissed her daughter, and then, to her amazement, noticed the little dents at the top of her ears. Jimmy would have a laugh over that one, she thought.

Abby had been able to finish out the school year, even in her condition. She had earned straight A's, and Virgil had taken her to a wonderful French restaurant in Monterey to celebrate. They had comfortably settled into married life, eagerly awaiting the birth. As promised, they flew to Twin Peaks and spent Thanksgiving with Abby's parents. It was during dinner that they had announced the pregnancy, and both Kenneth and Gretchen were pleased. They had taken an instant liking to Virgil, and knew that he was a good husband to Abby.

After dinner, Kenneth took Virgil out to the ranch to show him around, and Gretchen was pleased to be alone again with her daughter for the first time in three months. "So, when's the baby due?"

Abby paused for a moment, realizing that her answer would elicit more questions. "First week of May," she replied.

Her mother paused for a moment and said, "Abby, I have to ask you this, is Virgil the baby's father? With your not knowing him very long before getting married, it just wasn't like you to jump into something so serious."

Abby looked downward, then lifted her eyes to meet her mother's. "No," she replied. "It's Jimmy's baby, Mama. Virgil knew it before he proposed, and we don't want anyone else to know. We want to raise the baby as our own, and its last name will be Hobbs. Please promise me you won't tell anyone—please, not even Daddy."

"Okay, dear, but why didn't you tell me sooner?"

"I wanted to wait and tell you in person," replied Abby. "And I would have told you, even if you hadn't asked. We've never had secrets from each other, Mama, and that's the way it should always be."

Gretchen had begun to cry and reached over to give her daughter a hug. "You're a fine young lady, and I thank God everyday for blessing me with you," she said, holding Abby's face in her hands.

When Virgil, Abby, and Katie Rose left the hospital, Abby reflected on all that her mother meant to her and realized that she had some very large shoes to fill now that she had a daughter of her own. *I want only the very best for her*, she thought. *And someday, Katie, I may decide to tell you about your real father—maybe someday.*

Twenty-Eight

Katie Rose's parents had promised that for her tenth birthday, she could invite her friends over for a swim party. Five years ago, Virgil had built them a beautiful custom home in the upscale Seabright area of Santa Cruz. He and Abby had just finished having a heated swimming pool installed in their back yard, as Katie had become quite an accomplished swimmer. Since the age of four, she had belonged to the local swim team and had won several trophies. During the summer months, the family was busy with swim meets, often traveling out of the local area. Hazel was still in good health and would often accompany them, bragging to all the other parents about what a strong swimmer her great-granddaughter was.

On the morning of Katie's party, Abby was busily hanging decorations, and Virgil had gone to the store to buy groceries for the barbeque supper the girls would have after they finished enjoying the pool. He returned and helped Abby get everything ready for their daughter's special day.

They had built a good life—Abby had worked as a labor and delivery nurse for eight years at a local hospital in Santa Cruz, and Virgil's business continued to thrive. He now had ten employees, and most of his work had shifted to commercial construction. He had not yet been able to realize his dream of opening a surf shop and made the decision to postpone it until Katie was older. "I don't want to miss out on anything in her life," he'd said to Abby, knowing that owning another business would make substantially more demands on his time.

As the girls arrived for the party, Abby reflected on how much Virgil meant to her. She watched as he greeted his daughter's guests and escorted each one out to the pool. They ended the day with barbequed hot dogs, hamburgers, and Abby's great potato salad. Katie then blew out the candles of her cake, decorated in the shape of a lap pool. As they lay in bed that night, Abby thanked her husband for all of his help in giving their daughter a wonderful party and for being such a loving man.

The next day, Virgil kissed his wife goodbye as he did every morning before leaving. He had planned to spend a couple of hours surfing and as he drove away, she waved to him from the kitchen window.

Abby was just finishing the breakfast dishes when there was a knock at the door. She opened it to find their friend Bob Bailey, one of the local deputies, standing there. From the look on his face, she knew that he was about to give her some bad news.

"Can I come in?" he asked.

"Sure Bob," she said, feeling her heart begin to sink. "What's wrong—I mean you wouldn't be here like this if there wasn't something wrong."

"It's Virgil," he began. "You know that four-way stop at Seabright Drive. Well, there was a semi coming down the road, and his brakes went out. He couldn't stop and hit Virgil's car door, on the passenger's side. He died before the ambulance got there, Abby. I am so very sorry."

With her heart pounding and her head reeling, she sat down on the sofa and began sobbing hysterically. "Oh, God," she uttered when realizing that she now had to tell her daughter that her daddy was gone.

She thanked Bob, then held Katie Rose in her arms as she broke the news. The two sat locked together, crying for the next hour. She then went to the phone and called Virgil's family, then her own. Hazel came over immediately and spent the next few days helping out with whatever needed to be done and looking after Katie while Abby took care of all the funeral arrangements.

Gretchen flew out by herself to be with her daughter, as Kenneth had

passed away two years ago. Matthew, Nora and Cora arrived the morning of the funeral, and as their entire family entered the church for the services, Abby was not surprised to find it overflowing with all the people who had loved her husband. She invited everyone back to their home afterward, back to the beautiful home that Virgil had built for his family.

The guests had gone, and Gretchen was cleaning up in the kitchen. When her daughter came in, she walked over and took hold of Abby's hands. "I don't know what your plans are for the future, dear, but would you consider coming home to Twin Peaks for a little visit. I think it would do both you and Katie some good to get away for a bit. How about it?" Abby had taken a month's leave of absence from work and decided that her mother was right. It would be good to have a change of scene, get a new perspective, and decide what was best for she and Katie.

This house is so full of memories, she thought. So many memories. "I think you're right, Mama. We haven't been back to Twin Peaks in two years, and it will be good to see everyone again." She went upstairs, packed their luggage, and they all flew out together the next morning.

Twenty-Nine

Abby casually strolled the streets of downtown Twin Peaks. Not much had changed, and for that she was grateful. She walked past the Merc and smiled, remembering the day she had seen Jimmy staring at her in the window from across the street. She then made her way to Hopkins Diner and decided to go inside and have an early dinner. Might as well continue the walk down memory lane, she thought.

After opening the door, Abby looked around and realized that the entire restaurant had been re-furbished with new tables, chairs and curtains. It was done in Italian décor, complete with red and white checked linen tablecloths and candles.

"We don't open until five o'clock," said a man's voice from the kitchen. A familiar voice, she thought.

"Oh, I'll come back," she replied and suddenly Jim Riley came from the back up to the front of the restaurant.

"Abby!" he said, almost shrieking.

"Jimmy, Jimmy Riley" and before either of them were aware of it, found themselves in an embrace.

"What are you doing here?" she asked.

"I own it, didn't you see the sign out front?"

"It's just like you to name an Italian Restaurant "Riley's," she chuckled.

But Abby had to admit the place was beautiful. He had installed an elegant mahogany bar, with matching bar stools. There were mirrors on the back wall that reflected the lighted candles on the restaurant's tables. And, to top it all off, Puccini was playing in the background.

"Abby, I heard about your husband," said Jim. "I'm really sorry—heard he was a first-rate guy."

"Thanks Jimmy, that means a lot. And yes, he was a wonderful man," she said."

"Riley's" doesn't open for an hour. Will you join me for a drink, Abby?" he asked.

They sat at one of the tables, talking about all that had happened to each of them over the past eleven years. He told her about Fort Benning, and about seeing she and Virgil that day on the bench in Monterey when he had asked Abby to marry him. After two years at Fort Ord, he had been sent to Germany to finish out his tour of duty with the Army. After his discharge, he had lived in Italy and worked at an upscale Italian restaurant, learning all about the cuisine and restaurant management. It was while he was there that his father passed away, and eventually his mother's health was failing. He had returned to Twin Peaks eighteen months ago and cared for her until she died. Tom Hopkins had decided to sell the diner and Jim had bought it a year ago. It took six months to re-furbish and had been a success from the first day it had re-opened. There wasn't another Italian restaurant within fifty miles, and she could tell that he was a happy man, a mature man.

"Well, Jimmy Riley's grown up," she said, and they both smiled. She then proceeded to tell him everything about herself, too. About realizing her dream of becoming a nurse, her marriage to Virgil, raising Katie Rose, and what a wonderful daughter she was. As wonderful as her real father, she thought.

The time passed quickly, and before they knew it, the restaurant staff had arrived, ready for a busy Saturday night. They looked at Abby curiously, as they weren't aware that Jim had a girlfriend and it appeared that the two were somehow involved. Abby stood up to leave and Jim said, "Will I see you again before you head home to California?"

"Oh," she replied, "I'll be here a while longer. Do you have a phone? I was going to call Mama and ask her to drive Katie Rose over here so we could have dinner."

He flashed the big grin that she remembered from long ago and said excitedly, "That would be great, I'd love to meet her! You can use the phone in my office, right through those doors."

Abby and Katie were seated at the table studying the menu when Jim appeared in a white shirt, black bow tie and black pants. "May I take your order ladies?" he asked, looking amused.

"Katie, this is Mr. Riley…a dear friend of mine who just happens to own this restaurant."

"Nice to meet you, Mr. Riley," Katie said as she extended her hand.

God, she's beautiful—look at that red hair, just like her mother, he thought.

As he studied her, Abby suddenly realized that Jimmy was looking at Katie intently. Even in the dim candlelight, he saw the unmistakable dents in the top of her ears.

"What would you like to order honey?" she asked her daughter, attempting to break his fixation. "I'll have spaghetti and meatballs mom," she replied.

"And I'll have the same," said Abby, noticing that Jimmy was still focusing on Katie, realizing that he may be looking at his own daughter for the first time.

After dinner, Abby tucked her daughter into bed and found herself feeling agitated. What should I do, she wondered. Katie has only known one father, Virgil, and she loved him deeply. Now that he's gone, should I tell her about Jimmy? He's totally changed, she thought. God, since she last saw him, he had left the Army as a Sergeant, returned home to care for a dying parent, and become a successful business owner. Katie Rose could still have a father in her life—but what if telling her daughter was not the right thing? What if it damaged their relationship?

It was just past eleven o'clock and Abby realized there was one more place that she needed to visit. Gretchen had already gone to bed, and Abby grabbed a jacket and drove out to the lake.

It was once again a full moon and, as she remembered that night here years ago, was suddenly startled by the sound of a car approaching. The headlights dimmed and the car door opened. "I knew you'd be here," he said and she then realized it was Jimmy. He came nearer, into the moonlight.

"Abby," he said softly as he took hold of her hands and looked intently into her eyes. "I have to ask you something. Is Katie Rose my daughter?" She hesitated as her tears began falling. "Yes, Jimmy, she is. And I did what I felt was best for all of us back then."

He put his arms around her in a gentle hug.

"Someday we'll tell her, Jimmy, someday," she said. And at that moment, they both heard *Until We Meet Again* playing softly as a shooting star danced across the night sky.

Until We Meet Again

UNTIL WE MEET *Again*

About the Author

This is Elle Jameson Pearce's first book. She was previously a feature columnist who published six human interest articles for a local newspaper. Elle plans to continue writing romance books and also publish a children's series.
She resides in the beautiful state of Idaho.

PLEASE VISIT US AT
WWW.FACEBOOK.COM/ELLEJAMESONPEARCE

SETON
PUBLISHING

www.ingramcontent.com/pod-product-compliance
Lightning Source LLC
Chambersburg PA
CBHW060642130626
46555CB00002B/923